D1393256

SLOGGERS

SLOGGERS

Sid Waddell

BBC CHiLDReN'S BOOKS

This book is dedicated to the memory of
Jack Hill of Bowling Old Lane Cricket Club, Bradford

Published by BBC Children's Books,
a division of BBC Enterprises Limited,
Woodlands, 80 Wood Lane, London W12 0TT
First published 1994
© Sid Waddell 1994
ISBN 0 563 40301 2
Set in Sabon by Create Publishing Services Ltd, Bath
Printed and bound in Great Britain by Clays Ltd, St Ives plc
Cover printed by Clays Ltd, St Ives plc.

ONE

Slogthwaite Cricket Club, known throughout Lancashire as 'Sloggers', lies down a leafy lane near the centre
of Slogthwaite village. Local legend has it that a Viking
or Norseman called Slog settled in the clearing (thwaite)
by the river, and devised an early form of cricket, in or
around the year 890. Be that as it may, Sloggers is rich in
history, heritage and achievement. The walls of the
pavilion are hung with honours, and the ladies of the
club serve the best teas in Lancashire.

The local cricket fans are very broad-minded. They
even allow Yorkshire lads and lasses to play in their
teams. This sometimes causes problems.

Leonard Henry Higgs loved his mother Di to bits, but at
times like this she could be a real pain. It was the night
before the start of the new cricket season and Lenny
knew he should be in bed, dreaming of a victory over
Sloggers' arch-rivals, Dobcroft, in the match the next
day. But his mother had got twitchy at around nine
o'clock and now, forty-five minutes later, the entire
Higgs family was in the back garden playing a version of
floodlit cricket. 'Our Leonard needs the practice,' had
been Di's verdict. And she was – as usual – obeyed.

The Higgses' back garden in Rowmarsh Road, Slogthwaite, was not your run-of-the-mill place. The lawn
was marked out with white lines just like a cricket pitch.
In front of the compost heap at one end was a sight-
screen made out of canes and an old bedsheet. Chicken
wire protected the french windows at the opposite end.
The green-painted garden shed was hung with 'tins' of a
proper score-box and there was even an old Father Time
weathervane, exactly like the one at Lord's, on its lead
roof. The whole setup was a symbol of Di Higgs's
lifetime ambition – to get 'our Leonard' to follow in the

footsteps of Sir Leonard Hutton and play cricket for Yorkshire and England.

The focus of all this ambition yawned and settled into batting position at the compost-heap end. At the other end Barry Higgs, holding a storm lantern and three-year-old Geoffrey Higgs, dressed in pyjamas and dressing gown, acted as umpire. Demon fast bowler Di Higgs raced in to bowl.

'And it's a lovely night here at Sloggers,' Barry droned sarcastically, in a good imitation of the TV Test Match commentators. 'The unflagging Di Higgs hustles in from the Rowmarsh Road end. She's determined to suffer the batter to pace.' He raised his voice. 'Are you awake, young sir?'

The ball hit a divot and reared up on to Lenny's hip. He tried to fend it off defensively, mishit and dollied up a catch to his mother.

Up went Barry's finger. 'That's out. End of game. Well played. It's time for bed.' In his arms Geoffrey turned in his sleep.

Lenny tucked his bat under his arm, removed his gloves and began to trot towards the house. His stroppy mother grabbed him and, as usual when she was annoyed, let rip in broad Yorkshire.

'Hang about, our Leonard. Tha's not packing in yet. That straight drive still needs working on. It's not crisp enough.'

'It's a darned sight crisper than he is, dear,' said Barry. 'Dear' only slipped out when Barry was really cheesed off with his wife.

Di ignored Barry. She reached over to take the bat. 'Gimme that here and watch how the straight drive should be played.'

Lenny obeyed. Di marched to the wicket. Barry passed the lantern and the sleeping Geoffrey to Lenny. He rubbed the ball on his dressing gown.

'Knock her timbers over, Dad,' hissed Lenny under his breath.

'Fast as you like, Lankie,' yelled Di.

From a couple of houses up the street came a mournful wail. 'Why don't you Higgses shut up bawling and go to bed?'

'Soon,' shouted Barry as he raced in to bowl. Barry was no cricketer but desperation made him hurl a fast full toss at his wife. She played far too early and spooned the ball delicately back to Barry.

'Catch it! Catch it, Dad!' screamed Lenny.

Self-preservation deemed that Barry protect his teeth with his hands. The ball whacked into his palms. He winced with the pain but hung on.

'Howzat,' gasped Barry.

'That's out, Dad.' Lenny held up his forefinger and looked at his mother.

'Bad light! And it were a no-ball,' shouted Di. 'Hold that lantern higher, young Higgs.'

'You were out fair and square, dear,' said Barry. Lenny twigged that his dad had had enough. So Lenny did not raise his lantern.

Barry set his face and took Geoffrey from Lenny's arms. 'It is now time for bed, for all of us.' Di was obviously not happy but she followed Barry and Lenny through the french windows.

The room they entered, the Higgses' lounge, looked like a cross between a launderette, a sports shop and a table-top sale. White shirts, trousers and thick socks draped the radiators. A cricket video game was wired up to the television set and two of Lenny's cricket bats were propped up in the magazine rack near the door.

Di tried one last sally. 'About tactics tomorrow. Remember Dobby have a strong batting line-up...'

She got no further. Glaring at her as though she were an argumentative ten-year-old, Barry pointed through the open door to the stairs. 'Di, go to bed. Lenny, same – and if I catch you reading Boycott on Batting by torchlight under the covers, I'll have your guts for garters.'

This ended the discussion.

In fact Lenny was nowhere near asleep when he heard his parents close the door of their bedroom ten minutes later. It was not just worry about the cricket match that kept him awake. There was also the small matter of how to stash a violin well away from the eyes of his mother. Mrs Dorothy Ball, who taught Lenny music at school and privately, wanted her protégé to pile on the practice. So, in the morning, she was bringing round a school violin. Lenny had still not decided where in the house to hide it or where he could practise. He shuddered at the thought of his mother digging deep in a drawer or cupboard and finding the fiddle. She'd smash it to splinters, Lenny thought.

Lenny tossed in bed as Slogthwaite church clock banged out twelve-thirty. He sat up and switched on his bedside lamp. Seeking hope for the new season in memories of past triumphs, he let his tired eyes roam over his wall, covered in photographs of cricket teams he had played in since he was eight. His gaze settled on an older picture. It was yellowing and spotted with age. In gold italic print it bore the proud legend: 'Laston Recreation C.C. 1972'. In front of a wooden pavilion a team of brawny men stood smiling at the camera. Flared white trousers were in fashion, and so was shoulder-length hair. On the left-hand side of the team was a burly old man with a white beard. He was holding the hand of a bright-eyed girl of about twelve. Beneath them were the words: 'G.H. Stott, Chairman' and 'Diane Stott, tin-lass'.

The picture symbolised Di's obsession with cricket. Her grandfather, George Henry Stott, had been the W. G. Grace of the Barnsley Colliery League in the 1920s and 30s. Di had no brothers to continue in the family's cricketing tradition. But she had made sure that Lenny – named after Sir Leonard Hutton – and Geoffrey – named after 'Sir' Geoffrey Boycott – had been born in Yorkshire and been able to bat before they could walk.

Di knew that Lenny dabbled with the school fiddle. But if dabbling became 'interested', then, as they say in Yorkshire, 'the bricks would be down'. Nothing – animal, vegetable, or mineral – would be allowed to stand in the way of 'our Leonard' playing cricket for Yorkshire.

At least my dad's not obsessed by cricket, thought Lenny as sleep at last claimed him.

In the run-up to the cricket season Sloggers' coach, Stan Topping, had been trying to drill certain good qualities into his young charges. Responsibility. Common sense. Unselfishness. He had had some success with these. Punctuality, however, was a sore point at twelve-thirty on Saturday as preparations got under way for the match against Dobcroft. In fact only four of Stan's team had arrived at the appointed time, and they were now trying very hard to pull the ancient heavy roller along the square.

Adam 'Matey' Tait, so-called because he insisted on calling everyone 'matey' in his squeaky voice – even his headmaster at Slogthwaite Comprehensive – flopped on the grass after five minutes. He pulled a notebook from his pocket.

'It's no good us trying to pull together if two-thirds of the team is absent. So I'm starting the season's cricket fines here and now.' He began scribbling in the notebook.

Leroy 'Malcolm' Marshall, a West Indian lad who always wore muscle vests, flexed his pecs and pulled harder on the roller.

'Just you get back on this roller gang sharpish,' he shouted at Matey. 'We'll sort the rest out later.'

The two girls in the party nodded red-faced agreement. Unlike the two lads, Roz Crabtree and Zoë Milner were already in cricket whites because they had to get changed at home. 'Malcolm's right,' said Roz with the authority of a team vice-captain. 'Going on about fines is fine...'

Matey crowed with laughter. 'That's a ten-pence fine for an awful pun.'

'Shut it and pull,' screamed Zoë. She was a timid-looking girl but on occasions could tongue-lash with the best of them.

During the verbals a smart figure in a blue blazer, tie and creased grey flannel trousers had walked quietly to the edge of the square. He was now perusing *The Financial Times* and giving the odd bored look to the toilers on the roller.

'Stop posing with that pink paper and get grafting, Scooby,' Roz hissed.

Scooby did not look up. Apart from trying to make a fortune from making cricket bats in his shed, he had his eyes constantly on the stock market. 'I see AZP are up two points and Venezuela Consolidated are bullish,' he said loudly. His nickname came from his passion for Scooby-Doo doorstep sandwiches when he was younger. Along with Lenny Higgs, Scooby was the team's best batter.

A vision straight from Surf City came cruising over the grass. Jason Preston's choice of gear was as predictable as the path of an electric eel. Jason's image was now Beach Boys via New Kids with a dash of Hip Hop. He was sporting a pink baseball cap worn cockeyed, a pigtail, an earring in his right ear and a pair of black trainers the size of diving boots. He stopped and looked at the roller gang as though they were another species.

'Hang about, chaps and chapesses. I reckon you should be pushing this thing, not pulling it.'

Zoë tugged harder at the roller. 'If that's all you've got to say, pal, you can clear off and get changed.' She pointed at Jason's T-shirt which was like an explosion in a paint factory. 'Just looking at you makes me feel queasy.'

Jason went glassy-eyed with disdain and shuffled off.

'Ee, 'eck, I'm sorry I'm late.'

A gangly figure sprinted up to the square. He hurled

his cricket gear to the ground and began tugging manfully. 'Me bus 'ad to wait at the terminus for 'alf-hour. No driver. Honest.' These impassioned pure Lancashire tones were delivered by Balwinder – 'Bal' to all at Sloggers – Singh, a Sikh lad with a white topknot on his shiny black hair.

The rest of the roller gang were too shattered to question his alibi.

Ten minutes later the lads went off to get changed and Roz and Zoë, both in a full sweat with faces as red as beetroot, flopped on the bench by the score-box. It did them no good at all to see Donna Rothwell, the team's scorer, saunter up with her pencil case and scorebook, looking like a model from *Just Seventeen*.

'All ready for the new season, ladies?' Donna was her usual chirpy self.

Zoë's 'yes' was almost audible. Apart from Donna's stunning appearance, Zoë was always worried that one day Donna might pinch her place in the team. Roz would not even look Donna straight in the face. Roz had a real burner on Lenny Higgs and she saw Donna as Rival No. 1. Donna sussed the tension and breezed off into the score-box.

Ten minutes later the Sloggers' team, minus Lenny, were sitting outside the dressing room in blinding white cricket gear enjoying the April sunshine.

Ronnie 'Bugle' – cricket slang for 'slogger' – Banks had a colourful cycling hat perched on his head as usual. James Crann sat holding a new bat and looking as if he was about to face a firing squad. His nickname was 'Slasher' because he was precisely the opposite on the cricket field – the forward defensive shot was the only one he knew. Craig Spowart also wielded a posh new bat of willow. Craig was no good at batting, fielding or bowling, but some of the others fancied a go with his expensive bat so he was in the team.

Most of the opposition from Dobcroft were out on the pitch practising their fielding. They looked pretty slick, especially their captain, Ian Battersby, and their fast bowler, Ronnie Moss. No matter how high the team manager batted the ball, the Dobby lads took the catch cleanly and confidently.

Lenny's absence was beginning to provide more food for doubt. Stan was brooding inside the changing room. Scooby, who fancied being captain, summed up the touchy mood.

'Now what I'd like to know, fellow plebs, is where is our patrician captain, Sir Leonard Higgs?' Nobody said a peep. Scooby turned back to *The Financial Times*.

Lenny Higgs was going spare. It was half-past one, the game was due to start at two o'clock, and his mother was still nagging him about his straight drive.

'Please, Mum, let it drop,' Lenny pleaded as he put his bat into his coffin-style cricket bag. 'We should be at Sloggers now. I'm going to miss the team talk.'

Before Di could argue, Barry Higgs put his foot down. 'The lad's right. I'm driving off in the car in two minutes flat. Right?'

Di glared at them both. Without a word she raced upstairs.

'Gone for her binoculars, I'll bet,' Lenny sighed.

'Forget it and just do your best, son,' said Barry warmly.

The doorbell rang, loud and persistent. Like a jack rabbit Lenny hurtled out into the hall. He took his coffin because he had a fair idea who the caller was and he was right. Dot Ball handed over the school fiddle and she had to laugh as Lenny shoved it, case and all, down below his socks and boots to the bottom of the coffin.

'Can't talk now, Mrs Ball, I've got to get off to cricket.' Lenny desperately wanted her to go before his mother came down the stairs.

'OK,' said Dot. 'But don't just leave it there untouched. Practise!' She left sharpish, well aware of the tensions in the house. Lenny snapped down the catches of the coffin.

'I'm ready,' he yelled. 'Mum, are you hurrying up?'

His mum's feet clattered on the stairs.

The atmosphere in the Sloggers' dressing room could hardly have been worse. Stan had looked out of the window for a good thirty seconds while the team sat in silence. Matey had brandished the fines book ominously, but the rest had taken no notice. Stan, his face like thunder, turned to the team.

'Roz, stand by to toss up in a minute.'

Roz nodded. 'Right.'

Stan's voice was harsh and cracked, not its normal quiet tone. 'First game of the season. Dobby are a hard outfit. So I want effort, pride and, above all, common sense. I want no sloggers or dolly-drop bowlers in this team.'

The last remarks caused Bugle and Balwinder to shuffle. Both had been known either to lose concentration or to have mad rushes of blood in the heat of battle. Roz seethed with annoyance. She motioned to each of them to keep quiet.

The door flew open and Lenny tumbled in, his face red and his jacket off. He bundled his coffin under the bench and began to undress rapidly.

Roz and Zoë got up to leave. Stan looked round as if daring anyone to speak.

'Zoë and Roz, don't go – just turn your backs.'

There was a ripple of mirth. Matey sensed an opportunity. 'First fine of the season to L. Higgs. Ten pence for lateness.' There were more chuckles. 'And ten pence for undressing with ladies present.' The sombre mood broke.

'It was all my mum's fault,' pleaded Lenny as he laced up his boots.

'Gerraway,' said Stan. 'Go out and toss up as soon as you can.'

Matey elbowed through the noisy throng carrying a jester's cap and bells. He prodded Lenny in the chest. 'At

13

the moment you and your mother are even money to be Wally of the Day.'

Sloggers' tea-room, a partitioned-off section of the clubhouse, was as busy as the dressing room had been. Scooby's mother, Pat Masters, was dressed as if expecting royalty for potted-meat sandwiches and strong tea. Mary Pilling and Sharon Dempster cut, sliced and buttered, knowing that Pat was about to explode. Both ladies shuddered as Barry Higgs bounded in, happy as Larry, bearing a mountain of plastic food containers. Through the picture windows the track-suited Di could be seen on her hands and knees peering at the wicket.

'It's revolution time, ladies.' Barry had apparently not noticed the witch-like scowl on Pat Masters' face. Barry plonked his load on the counter. He burbled on, 'I've often thought teas here at Sloggers, though substantial, lacked a bit of sparkle. So I've brought peppers and sweetcorn and I've made garlic sausage rolls to liven up the fare. What do you reckon?'

The chopping and spreading ceased. Sensing the atmosphere, little Geoffrey huddled behind his dad's legs. Pat Masters sneered at Barry's boxes.

'This is no time for joking, Mr Higgs. Peppers and garlic – in cricket teas? Whoever heard of such nonsense?'

There was a clatter of young feet in trainers. Roz, Zoë, Scooby, Matey and Balwinder rushed through the door.

'Got any pop ...' was all Matey managed to blurt out before Roz twigged the scene and shut him up. The kids looked round wide-eyed as Di Higgs trotted past them towards the counter. One look from Pat stopped Di in her tracks.

'You should have been here for tea-duty nearly an hour ago, Mrs Higgs.' Pat's voice could have stripped paint. 'You and I are on that list – ' Pat pointed to the club notice-board – 'as tea-ladies of the day.'

14

Di had paced several metres to the counter. Red-faced, she was obviously trying to retain a droplet of cool. 'I'm sorry, Mrs Masters. I completely forgot. You see, Yorkshire could well hear about Lenny so I was checking the pitch...'

Pat did not utter a sound. She dropped her eyes from Di's and with a nod to Sharon and Mary began cutting and buttering. Di looked helplessly at Barry. The Sloggers' kids huddled together near the door like sheep awaiting a Pennine blizzard.

'Let's get out of here,' whined Matey.

'Hang on.' Roz sensed a clash of wills about to take place.

Barry forced a wink at Di. He pulled a pinny from the drawer and theatrically put it on. 'Only one solution to this, ladies.' He began taking his garlic stuff from the boxes. 'I shall represent the Higgs family on teas this season. While my good lady trains her binoculars on our Lenny. OK?'

Pat let out a hiss like a bicycle tyre going over sharp tacks. She tore off her pinny and flung it across the counter. Sharon and Mary stopped working. Pat rounded on Barry. 'I have had enough. In my fifteen years on teas here at Sloggers no man has ever been behind this counter. No mother has ever skived off with the excuse that her son's cricket must be monitored every second. No one has mocked our food or threatened to put garlic or other muck in it.'

Pat was now halfway to the door. She had one parting shot. 'And your son should not be team captain. My Timothy should.'

Scooby cringed at this. Nice one, Mother, he thought.

The kids crowded round Barry who was looking happy but bemused.

Di, as usual, bounced back as if nothing had happened. 'We could have the game won in an hour and a half, so let's forget about tea.' She breezed out.

Zoë looked shell-shocked. 'No tea. But I had no dinner 'cos I was so nervous.'

15

Roz had been weighing up the situation with a sombre face. She called the others into a huddle. After a minute's whispering she left the others giggling.

'Don't worry, Mr Higgs.' Roz winked. 'Do your best, and something might turn up.'

'Hurry, Roz,' yelled Scooby. 'They're about to toss up.'

All the kids ran out, leaving Barry looking at twelve garlic sausage rolls and twelve drop scones. He was thinking about the Bible story of the loaves and the fishes.

TWO

Lenny Higgs was mightily confused. Normally tossing up was a lonely experience. If you won, a million maybes shot through your brain. What if the pitch turns? What if it rains? What if I elect to bat and we go to pieces? Today, however, as he stood in the middle of the pitch with Ian Battersby, the Dobby skipper, Lenny had more advisers round him than a minister at the United Nations. Stan rarely told Lenny what to do. But there had been overnight rain, so Stan's thoughtful look might mean field. Di stood behind Stan at the edge of the square making bowling motions which meant field, if you can. Lenny tossed the ten-pence piece.

'Heads,' shouted Ian.

Roz, Zoë, Scooby, Matey and Balwinder dived down to see what side was up.

'Tails,' screeched Roz.

'Tails,' bellowed Scooby. 'You must bat.'

The five of them mobbed Lenny. 'Bat! Bat!' they yelled.

Stan marched off to the dressing room. Di, for once, was silent.

Ian looked drily at Lenny. 'What do you say, Len?'

As Lenny opened his mouth, Scooby whispered in his ear, 'Track's a beaut, skip. Me and you will make hay.'

'We'll bat,' said Lenny firmly.

Five minutes later, as he finished strapping on his pads, Lenny began to think his team-mates had been out in the sun too long. His five advisers, who normally begged to go high in the batting order, regardless of form, were all begging to go well down. Roz, who was helping Bugle to get padded up, explained the logic behind the idea.

'Because of all the rain recently, nobody's had batting practice. So why not use today to let the tail-enders, middle order and yahoo-merchants like Bugle here get a feel of leather on willow?'

Bugle coloured at being so described but kept his trap shut. In his wildest dreams he had never opened the batting for Sloggers.

Scooby chipped in his twopennyworth. 'So, if you and Bugle get around thirty quickly, Jason can be number three...'

Jason, who was wildly superstitious, beamed. 'Three is fine. My unlucky numbers in the present phase of the moon are five and seven. Mind, if there's magpies about it will be a different matter. As you know, they are mega bad luck.'

Lenny got the drift. 'Right, Bal, you're number four.'

Bal frowned. 'No, I'm not whacking t'owld leather as hard as I'd like. Put Malcolm in before me.'

Lenny thought there was something odd about Bal's tone, but Malcolm was overjoyed. 'Bal, yer a pal.'

He picked up one of the club's old bats and began practising shots that would have made Geoffrey Boycott tear his hair out.

There was a sharp rap on the door. Lenny and Bugle leapt to their feet, bats gripped firmly. Stan, wearing a white umpire's jacket, put his head round the door.

'Right?' Stan asked, with a look of concern at Bugle.

'Right, boss,' said Lenny. He pointed to Bugle. 'Opening with a bang.'

Stan nodded but did not smile.

A joky round of applause sent Lenny and Bugle out to face Dobby.

The first over, from Ronnie Moss, was extremely quick. Lenny blocked the first three balls, drove the fourth past mid-off, and the batsmen ran one. In the score-box Donna put down her coloured pencils and hid her eyes as Ronnie unleashed a bouncer at Bugle. Bugle's shot would have pleased a hammer thrower. The ball reared off the edge of his bat and flew over the clutching hands of the slips for a very lucky four.

Outside the score-box Scooby, Roz and Matey cheered. 'That's the way, Bugle. Give him some pasty, matey,' cried Matey. Zoë ran into the score-box and whispered something to Donna. She ran out quickly. Donna watched the next ball carefully. It nearly knocked the bat from Bugle's grip. But the ball rolled gently down the wicket.

'Not a bad start, five runs for nowt,' said Donna to Nidge, her ten-year-old assistant. She stood up and gestured to him to take her place. 'Look after the book – neatly. I'll be back in ten minutes.' Nidge was a quiet, obedient lad who wanted to be a real scorer when he grew up. He obeyed. Donna flitted down the steps and over the wall behind the score-box.

Roz, Scooby, Zoë and Matey were walking around the ground trying to look nonchalant.

'Leather it, Len,' shouted Scooby as the group neared the old seat, eighty metres along the boundary from the score-box. Di Higgs stood erect in her usual place by the seat. On it Mr Joe Ackroyd, eighty-three years of age, a man who had never raised his voice in all those years, sat with his dog and waited – for the loudest voice in East Lancashire.

'That's right,' Di roared, looking at Scooby. 'Hit the bad balls, our Leonard.'

Leonard prodded Ian Battersby's first two seamers back to him and then cracked a lovely four straight past the bowler. Di began to applaud and turned to Zoë and Co. Scooby had disappeared.

'Where's Scooby?' asked Di.

Roz chose to misunderstand. 'Oh, he's batting down the order. We've decided to mix it up a bit today. Sloggers and strokers alternate all the way down. Worth a try.'

Di gave a humph and trained her binoculars on the action. Lenny played and missed. The ball hit his pads. 'Howzat!' yelled the Dobcroft team as one man.

'Not out, you idiots,' Di screamed.

The kids and Mr Ackroyd went walkabout. Zoë shot off behind the practice nets and disappeared through a hole in the hedge. Roz and Matey slunk out of the main gate.

Outside the dressing room, Jason sat mournfully in his pads. He had all his fingers crossed and was keeping a sharp eye out for magpies. He turned to ask Bal's advice, but Bal too had gone missing. In the middle Bugle clouted a ball at the fielder at mid-on. The kid dived out of the way to stop being decapitated.

'Play right in yer head, Bugle,' pleaded Jason.

Something fluttered in the hedge behind him. Ashen-faced, fingers apart, he sighed with relief, the 'thing' flapping in the hedge was only a black bin liner. Jason put his shades on.

Di, on a nervy tour of the pitch, snarled at him. 'Get those silly sunglasses off, lad. You're in next, though heaven knows why. You should be letting your eyes get used to normal light so you can judge the speed of the ball properly.'

Jason, in pleasant, calming gloom, ignored her.

After six overs Sloggers were doing well, even if most of both Lenny's and Bugle's shots had been lucky, to say the least. The score was now 21 for 0. After his initial rush of blood, Bugle had retreated into his shell. He paddled two balls of very little pace tamely back to Ian, the bowler.

'Billy, try and spin this lot out,' Ian yelled as he tossed the ball to a skinny lad.

Ian sneered at Lenny. 'When are the lasses coming in to bat, Higgsy? They can't do any worse than you two.'

Lenny ignored the crack. He walked down the wicket to Bugle. 'You're going great. Keep this end up and I'll get after the spinner.'

'Right, skip.' Bugle tilted his cycling cap to a jauntier angle and sat on the splice of his bat.

Three balls later the jauntiness was gone. Bugle tried to swipe the ball to the boundary, but it simply flew up for an easy catch to the wicket-keeper. Bugle shrugged and began to trudge off. Jason stood up, removed his shades and began to tremble like a malaria victim. Malcolm grabbed him. 'What's up? Nerves?'

'No, magpies!' whispered Jason.

A brainwave hurtled into Malcolm's mind. He rushed into the dressing room, rummaged in Jason's cricket bag, and pulled out a coloured bandana. Quick as a flash he wrapped it round Jason's eyes and began leading him to the wicket.

'What's the game, blind man's buff?' asked Ian.

'André Agassi, as I live and breathe,' quipped Ronnie. He shouted, 'Wrong bat, André.'

Even Stan had to chuckle as Malcolm unwrapped the bandana, and Jason took guard. 'Middle stump, please, aaaagh!' Jason pointed, eyes blazing, at a fat magpie that had just landed beyond slip. He began saluting the bird with his left hand and chanting, 'Good morning, Mr Magpie,' while holding the bat with his right. The spinner ran in, bowled a good ball, and Jason, single-handed, whacked the ball over the slip. The ball raced to the boundary, with all the Dobby lads screaming, 'Run!' after the fielder. Upset by all the yelling, the magpie flew off lazily. The ball rolled gently over the boundary for four.

'Great shot,' laughed Lenny. 'Now trust your luck.' He looked across at the clubhouse and was delighted to see Scooby and Roz walking out with his dad and Geoffrey to watch the game. Lenny had seen the group disappear earlier, but now he relaxed. If he was out now, Roz, Scooby or one of the rest would take the strain.

'Come on, Lenny. Let's see your strokes,' yelled Barry. Just before Lenny got set to face the next over, it crossed his mind that his father did not seem upset about the tea fiasco. He must have given up the ghost, thought Lenny. From the corner of his eye he saw Matey and Zoë bustle past Barry with a bin liner. The ball was a good one. It pitched on length and lifted a bit. Lenny steered it towards point.

Jason, full of himself after a fluky four and three dead-bat prods, screamed, 'Yes.'

Lenny looked up. Jason was a couple of metres away from him and swooping like a seagull. 'No,' screamed Lenny. He held up his hand like a policeman on point duty. It was hopeless. The bowler whipped off the bails with Jason miles out. There was a deafening silence as he trudged off. The ancient pulleys and tins in the score-box clanked to 27 for 2.

As Malcolm paraded out, swinging the bat like a battle-axe, Ian Battersby strolled past Lenny. 'I told you to bring them lasses in. Your blokes are useless wimps.'

Lenny was about to riposte, but a movement by the score-box took his eye. Donna scrambled over the wall with a rucksack. Puzzled, Lenny settled at the crease. The ball wanted smacking. It bounced just short of a length, sat up, begged ... then a cry from the boundary erupted like Vesuvius. 'Cream it, our Leonard, cream it!'

Lenny played the shot straight, but the shout fazed him. He lost power. The ball flew a metre off the ground straight back to the bowler. It whacked into his hands. 'Howzat,' he moaned in pain.

Stan's fingers went up and his mouth went down at the edges. 27 for 3 was the score and Sloggers were in deep trouble.

Two minutes later Roz stood with Scooby, Zoë and Matey outside the dressing room. Lenny had disappeared inside and was obviously stewing. In the middle Craig was surviving against some hostile fast bowling from Ronnie.

'I could strangle Mrs Higgs,' snarled Scooby. 'I reckon Len was about to cut loose when her gob stepped in.'

Roz came to a decision. 'As vice-captain I am going in to get padded up. Also, to calm Lenny down.'

'Sound idea, matey,' said Matey.

Lenny did not look as dejected as Roz had expected. He had taken his pads off and was putting his bat back in his coffin. With a guilty start, he slammed down the lid when he spotted Roz. He gave a weak laugh. 'We need a miracle, Roz.'

She wanted to give him a cuddle but it was a time for professionalism. 'Your mother being muzzled would be a start!'

Lenny sighed. 'It'll always happen. She wants me to do well, so she goes OTT.' A flicker of aggression crossed his good-natured face. 'Mind, I was a bit distracted by you, Scooby and Co, sloping off and back.'

Roz reddened. 'Just to get sweets, pop and crisps.' She looked away from him. 'Most probably we'll get no tea 'cos of the strike, so folks must fend for themselves.'

'Get your pads on then, Crabtree.' Lenny at last managed a real smile. 'We're not beat yet.'

His mother entered like Darth Vader with toothache. 'Our Leonard, that were the sloppiest shot tha's ever played.'

Roz stopped fastening her pads. 'With due respect, Mrs Higgs, this is no time for an inquest. We are in mid-match and we want to win it. So please, if you want to bawl and shout, do it elsewhere. Preferably out of earshot of those playing in this game.'

The barb struck deep. Di turned crimson. She pulled the zip of her Yorkshire CC track suit up to her throat. She wheeled to the door. 'I still reckon you should have fielded!' Di spat the words out. Then left.

Lenny and Roz fell into each other's arms laughing. 'If my mother was sitting in the electric chair she'd insist they were switching it on wrong,' laughed Lenny.

'Are we interrupting something?' Scooby was back in sarcastic mode.

'A very fineable offence. Snogging in the changing room,' said Matey, fines book at the ready.

A 'Howzat!' echoed from the middle. 'Craig's out,

caught,' shouted Zoë. Slasher, in helmet and pads, stuck his face around the door. 'Do I have to go in now, skip? It's muck or nettles time and I feel awful.'

'No sweat, Slash,' said Roz. 'Take a stroll round to calm your nerves. I'll go in.' She finished fastening her pads.

As she clattered to the door Lenny patted her on the back. 'Go on, show Bigmouth Battersby what a "girl" can do.'

Matey piped in. 'I'll let yer off the snogging fine if you get a fifty.'

'Done,' said Roz, glowering with concentration. She glanced up at the score-box. It read 32 for 4. Donna poked her head out of the hatch and gave her a thumbs-up. 'Give 'em some pasty, Roz.'

Battersby's reception committee out in the middle had obviously never heard of gentlemanly conduct. Ian brought in three slips and stationed Ronnie at suicide point, about a metre from the bat. 'Just think of playing rounders, dearie,' sneered Ronnie. 'Pat the ball gently to me.'

Roz looked him straight in the teeth. 'You,' she said, 'will need a helmet – or intensive care.'

She was not kidding. The first ball would have broken Ian's ankles, had he not leapt in the air like a Cossack dancer. The ball flew to the boundary to Sloggers' cheers. Ronnie berated the bowler. And Ian threatened to chin Ronnie.

Roz winked at Stan. 'Nice of these Dobby lads to give me an easy ball to get cracking,' she said loudly.

Di was still so het up at Lenny's failure that she could not stand seeing the team or Roz do well. As Roz continued to flay the bemused Dobby attack, Di entered the tea-room. Barry had spotted her striding towards the clubhouse, and was now standing outside the closed sliding doors of the tea section, holding Geoffrey. He seemed very twitchy.

'Bit of a turnabout, isn't it, love?' asked Barry, too brightly.

'Yes,' said Di. 'We could do with tea soon. We'll probably make ninety. But it won't be enough. Tea would have given Stan and me time to calm them down and think about tactics to force a draw.'

Barry looked crafty. 'Spread the word that there will be cold drinks *only* after our innings. Then mebbe I'll manage a cuppa, and the odd bag of crisps at the end.'

Di looked suspiciously at the partition. 'Fancy a brew now?'

Barry jumped. 'No! No! Look.' He pointed through the picture window. Roz was down on one knee and the ball was disappearing over the clubhouse. It rattled on the slates above them. Stan's arms raised high to signal a six-hit. Barry bustled Di through the door. 'We've got to be outside for this, dear. Roz is going bananas.'

Di gave a slight grin. 'Mebbe we *can* do better than a draw.' She followed him out. 'Play right in yer head, Roz, don't thrape that leather, stroke it!' The voice could have been heard over the Pennines in Barnsley.

There were smiling Sloggers' faces all round the ground as Slasher and Bal faced the very last over. Scooby had cracked a breezy thirty; Roz had made forty-two; and now the score was 115. Dobcroft had got over their patch of arguing in lumps with each other, and were back on the put-the-opposition-off trail.

'Bloomin' stupid hat,' shouted the keeper as Bal faced Ronnie's first ball. Bal whacked the ball for four. He tapped his topknot. 'Bloomin' stupid *ball*, pal.'

Bal swiped wildly at the next four balls as Di screamed, 'Hit out or get out,' from the boundary. Nobody minded her mouthiness now. Bal was doing the right thing. Ball five flew off the bat over the slips for another four. Then Bal pushed a cheeky single off the last ball. 124 for 7 rattled up in the frame as Slasher and Bal walked off. Lenny led the Sloggers' applause.

Di held up her hands before the teams went into the changing rooms. 'The bad news, folks, is that there is no

25

tea today.' There were groans all round. But Lenny thought he saw Roz pitch a crafty wink at Scooby. Di continued: 'But there's drinks for you all now.'

Bugle waved his cycling cap in front of his face. 'But, Mrs Higgs, me belly thinks me throat's cut.'

'Tough,' said Di and she jogged off towards the club-house. Outside, Pat Masters, Sharon and Mary sat looking like the Spanish Inquisition. Di gave them the snake eyes. 'The team are doing well. No thanks to some.' Pat coloured up but decided to say nowt.

A few minutes later Stan was ending a short team talk in the dressing room as Di came in with a tray of drinks.

'... so though a hundred and twenty-four is probably not quite enough against Dobby, go for it. Pressurise them,' said Stan. 'Use all your bowlers, Lenny. Spin might be the answer.'

'Rubbish,' hissed Di. 'There's no spin in that wicket.'

Lenny's voice was dry as a bone. 'That's not what you said two hours ago, Mother.'

Giggles started, but Stan held up his hand for hush. 'Any road up, Len, this lot are cocky. They might do summat daft against Bal and Zoë.'

'Zoë! With her little donkey drops.' Di looked at Stan as though he had lost his marbles. 'Don't be a complete wassock, Stan.'

It was below Stan's dignity to reply, but Matey was in like a rocket. He brandished the fines book. 'I'm sorry, Mrs Higgs, but you've pushed me to this.'

'What?' asked Di.

'I'm fining you for two serious offences.' All the faces in the room, except Di's, were now beaming. Matey licked his pencil. 'First offence. Shouting at our skipper and getting him out. Ten pence.'

There was a couple of 'hear, hears'.

'Don't be silly,' Di blustered.

Matey held up his pencil. 'And ten pence for calling our manager a wassock.'

There was a ripple of applause. Di fished in her

pockets and handed Matey twenty pence. 'I'll support any scheme that keeps you lot interested in cricket. Who else has been fined?'

'Jason for saluting a magpie,' Matey intoned. 'Lenny for being late, and Lenny and Roz for snogging in here.'

'Snogging! Leonard, what's this about ...' Di got no further. All the glasses were empty.

Stan glowered at Di. 'Now we've all supped up, can we *shut* up and play cricket?'

Lenny rushed out at the head of the team.

The first half-hour of the Dobcroft innings was a nightmare for Sloggers. Ian and Ronnie had come out grimfaced and were playing right in their heads. The first three Sloggers' bowlers were not. Malcolm tried to bowl too fast. Slasher could not get his run-up right. Scooby kept bowling full tosses. After eight overs the score was 52 for 0. In desperation Lenny put Bal in to bowl.

Di was standing on the boundary by the old seat. Mr Ackroyd, cotton wool in his ears, was sitting down. And Matey was fielding a couple of metres away from them. Di had been too sloughened off to shout. Another four fizzed past Matey.

'At this rate they're not going to need thirty overs. They'll knock the runs off in fifteen,' Di erupted.

Matey wagged his finger at her. 'I should fine you again for having no faith.' In fact, he had very little left himself. The only happy Sloggers' face was on Barry. Still in his pinny, and with Geoffrey holding his hand, he stood in the clubhouse door. 'Come on, Sloggers,' he yelled. 'Keep yer heads up.'

'He obviously has no idea of the trouble we're in,' sniffed Di. For some reason Matey was grinning now, and giving a thumbs-up to Barry. 'Loopy,' Di sighed.

At the end of Bal's over Dobcroft were 62 for 0. Ian and Ronnie stood in the middle of the wicket chatting casually, while Lenny looked at the ball as though it were crystal. At first he thought of trying his own tweakers, but shuddered at the thought of what might happen if he was not spot on. Thanks a bunch, Higgsy.

Roz had moved up to him. 'Try Zoë,' she whispered.

Bal heard this. He began to shake. His next ball was delivered from a metre behind the line and it pea-rolled up to Ronnie. By the end of the next over Bal was a nervous wreck and Dobby were on sixty-nine.

There was a deathly silence round the ground as Lenny rubbed the ball on his trousers. 'Zoë, I want you.'

The silence became thick with whispers.

'I can't watch,' hissed Di to Mr Ackroyd.

'This could be fun,' murmured Donna.

But the loudest, most strained sounds came from Dobcroft. 'It's a girl.' 'The *girl's* going to bowl.' 'Whack it, Ian.' The latter forty per cent bravado; sixty per cent hope.

What Roz and Lenny knew about Zoë that others did not was that, though she seemed a timid girl, she had enormous powers of concentration. It had taken her to the top in ballet class. She frowned and slowly measured her run-up. She licked the first two fingers of her right hand. Ian, face locked in a sneer, held the bat like a club. Zoë gave the ball lots of air. Ian stepped down the wicket. His cow-shot missed the ball. Bugle whipped off the bails. Up went the finger.

As Sloggers mobbed Zoë, the Dobcroft batters' faces turned a whiter shade of pale. 'Ian, diddled by a *girl*,' whined the next man in. Donna rattled the score up to 69 for 1.

The next lad in could hardly get to the crease for Sloggers' fielders. Lenny had them crowding the bat like Apaches round a wheel-less wagon train.

The new batter tried a swipe. The ball ricocheted off Matey's helmet at suicide point and rolled back towards Zoë. Ronnie was halfway down the track yelling, 'Run.' His partner froze. Zoë whipped off the bails.

'Pillock,' screamed Ronnie at the other batter. Zoë pointed demurely to the changing room.

Lenny completed the psychological blitz by bringing Roz on at the other end. In ten minutes Dobby were all out for 103 runs, most of them fluked, edged or slogged.

'Who needs tea after a victory like that?' An excited Lenny stood in the changing room.

'Me for one,' said Zoë with a sly grin.

'Me too,' said Scooby.

'Let's see if Bazza can oblige,' said Matey.

The three of them, accompanied by Roz, shot out. Lenny watched them race over the pitch to the club-house. 'Stark, raving mad,' he sighed and finished drying his hair.

A quarter of an hour later there was a very strange, strained atmosphere in the tea section of the club-house. The two teams sat at opposite sides of the room. Sloggers could hardly stop laughing and crowing about the victory. Lenny looked round. There was no sign of Scooby, Matey, Roz, Zoë or Donna.

Dobby sat tight-lipped, as did Pat Masters, Sharon and Mary. Di stood glum-faced, looking out of the window. Only Stan and Arthur, the Dobby manager, were cool. They sat chinwagging merrily. On the tables were empty plates and cups. But nothing to put on or in them.

Suddenly a metre gap appeared in the partition and Roz led out the other four. All were carrying pots of tea. As they set them on the tables, Barry stepped out looking like the cat who got the cream. Behind him Geoffrey burbled in a very excited manner.

'Right,' shouted Barry as Roz and Co returned to the platform. 'Tea is served.'

To gasps of wonder, Matey and Scooby pushed back the partition to reveal the best spread ever seen at Slog-gers. Adult eyes goggled and the kids began to lick their lips.

Roz and the rest took up position behind the counter. She began to shout like an ace bingo-caller! 'Hot garlic

29

sausage rolls. Salad with walnuts and peppers. Tripe with pineapple. Tuna with banana.'

The kids of both sides needed no urging. They tucked in like gannets. Bal was given the special tea of tuna; Di and Stan tucked in with a laugh and a shake of the head. 'Where on earth did it all come from?' asked Di. Barry tapped his nose. Roz gave him an outrageous wink.

Pat and her two cronies refused to partake. They sat and glared at Barry as though he had proposed a session of devil worship.

In no time, the food was gone. 'Best cricket tea I've ever had,' said Ian Battersby to Barry.

'You ain't seen nothing yet,' said Barry with a cool grin. 'Who's for hot chocolate fudge cake?' It was not a joke. As Roz and her team served the throng Pat, now shame-faced, walked up to the counter.

'Try some, Mum,' said Scooby cheekily. 'It's smashing.'

Pat accepted a morsel. 'Excellent,' she exclaimed as she tasted it. 'Barry, I want to apologise to you and your wife. This is a first-class tea. Consider us again your colleagues, if you will.'

Di had moved up behind her. She nodded to Barry. 'No probs, Mrs Masters. Apology accepted.'

'Can I have the recipe for this delicious fudge cake?' asked Pat. 'I have a batch at home in my freezer. But this is better.'

Barry froze. He looked at Scooby who shrugged. Di noticed that all of Roz's gang now looked very twitchy. Pat moved off. Di twigged. 'Barry Higgs. Don't tell me that the chocolate fudge cake, and all the rest of this food was...'

'Borrowed,' said Roz softly.

'Given to a needy cause,' said Zoë.

'I did have a strike on my hands, dear, and twenty-two hungry kids,' said Barry lamely.

Di began to grin. 'I've been fined twenty pence today for opening my big mouth. I don't know what you deserve, Barry Higgs.'

'A medal,' quipped Matey. 'And five stars off Egon Ronay.'

Since the traditions of Oliver Twist, and his 'I want some more' lark, are natural to any kind of kids, it is no surprise that even after a slap-up tea some could find room for food.

Bugle and Jason had been foraging in a corner of the kitchen area.

'What's this?' asked Jason. He pulled a big cardboard box out from under the sink.

'Smells ace,' said Bugle. He lifted the box on to the counter. All the team crowded around.

Bugle opened the lid to reveal well over a dozen newly baked pork pies. He tried one.

'Perfect!' sighed Bugle smacking his lips.

'But where did they come from?' asked Roz.

Jason scratched around in the bottom of the box and pulled out a tatty note. Printed in big capital letters was the message: HOPE YOU ENJOY THESE SNACKS. THE PIE PIPER IS ON YOUR TRACKS.

'The Pie Piper! Who's he?' asked Matey.

'Tricky – but talented,' said Bugle wiping crumbs from his chops.

'Disgusting,' said Pat Masters.

THREE

The Sloggers' team thought they had a free weekend a week after the Dobcroft match, but Stan thought otherwise. 'You lot have a long way to go in all departments before you frame up to my standards,' had been Stan's last words after the cordon bleu tea. 'So I want you all here for special practice at noon next Saturday.'

There had been a few grimaces and groans. But in their hearts the whole team knew that good luck and a loss of bottle by Dobby had won them the game.

Saturday dawned bright and warm. At 10.30 Donna Rothwell was finishing her violin practice in Dot Ball's house. The window of the living-room was open and the garden echoed to bird-song. Now and again the bushes rustled.

'Have you got rats out there?' Donna asked Dot.

Dot laughed. 'Not that I know of.' Dot's face turned serious. 'I gave Lenny the school violin a week ago to practise when he could. Has he been doing?'

It took a few seconds for Donna to answer. 'Well, after the game last week me and him did pop into the score-box for a bit of practice. Roz Crabtree looked as though she wanted to garrotte me. She's nuts on Lenny, you see – thinks he's drop-dead gorgeous – but . . .'

'Score-box!' exclaimed Dot. 'Why the score-box?'

''Cos Di Higgs would throw a blue fit if she knew Lenny had the fiddle. She thinks he should give up practising totally. Gets in the way of his cricket, you see.' Donna lapsed into broad Yorkshire. 'It's me lad's destiny to laik cricket for Yorkshire and England, aye, by 'eck it is an' all.'

Dot did not laugh. 'So Lenny carts the fiddle around in his cricket coffin and practises when he can.'

'That's right,' sighed Donna.

'So most likely he's *not* going to turn up for his lesson

at ten-thirty?' She looked at her watch. 'He's five minutes late now.'

Donna packed up her gear.

'How's your cricket going, love?' asked Dot. 'I remember when I used to play at school. Are you in the team?'

'No,' said Donna. 'I'm still the scorer. But I'll get in if it kills me.'

Donna was halfway down the path when she heard a loud rustle in a rhododendron bush. As she stopped a low voice echoed out. 'Donna! Donna! In here, quick.' The voice, the eyes, and the face peeping out of a bobble hat were those of Leonard Henry Higgs. Stifling a laugh Donna joined him, under cover of the bushes. He was wearing a track suit and had his cricket coffin with him.

'Stop laughing, woman,' hissed Lenny. 'This is getting beyond a joke. My mum thinks I've gone out with my coffin to get new grips put on my bats for the practice. And I've twice been asked if I'm a *ventriloquist*.'

Donna began to shake with laugher.

'You're all right,' said Lenny rather peevishly. '*Your* mum won't have spies on your tail. If *my* mum hears tell of me within half a mile of this house I'm ancient history.'

Donna stuck her head out of the street side of the bush. 'Coast clear, Bond. Proceed with mission.'

'See you in an hour at the end of Green Lane,' whispered Lenny as he broke cover and pelted to Dot Ball's door. 'Your turn for the sweets.'

Roz Crabtree was about to blow her cool. She and Zoë had been ringing the Higgses' doorbell for nearly five minutes but they'd had no joy. Odd shouts were coming from the back garden, so somebody was in. Both girls were in track suits for the practice, and Roz held a bundle of envelopes.

'Stick one through. Lenny'll get it,' said Zoë.

'No,' said Roz coyly. 'I want to put this invitation into his hands.'

'And see the light of love in his eyes. Mills and Boony, swoony-swoony,' giggled Zoë.

Roz just glared at her and punched the bell. Within ten seconds the door was opened by Barry Higgs. Roz pulled out one of the envelopes and offered it to Barry.

'Don't say that I've been selected for the team.' Barry grinned.

Roz blushed. 'This is an invitation for Lenny to come to my birthday party next Saturday. It's in the club-house after the game.' A frown crossed her face. 'Mrs Higgs will let him come, won't she?'

A voice that could have stripped paint echoed from the garden. 'Barry! Barry! Stop skiving and get back out here.'

Barry winked at Roz. 'Why not step out on to the turf at Lord's and ask her yourself?' He pointed to the girls' cricket bags. 'Leave them here or she'll have you out polishing up your forward defensives.'

Roz left Lenny's invitation on the hall table and they all went out on to the lawn.

A 'Timeless Test' was in progress. Little Geoffrey was at the wicket with a cut-down wooden bat, cardboard shinguards sellotaped to his legs and a floppy David Gower sun-hat.

Di was bowling spinners to him with a semi-hard corky ball. She was in no mood for social niceties. 'If you want to gab you'll have to help out,' said Di. She pointed to the score-board on the shed that showed Geoffrey's score of ninety-one. 'Zoë, you be scorer. Roz, field at silly mid-on. Barry, long-on. Behind me.'

The girls and Barry did as they were told. Barry coughed to attract Di's attention. 'Er – Roz is having a party, dear . . .'

Di took not a blind bit of notice. She'd pitched a ball well up to Geoffrey. The little lad swished his bat and missed it. Di shouted at him as though he'd mugged his grandma. 'What have I told you about wafting, our Geoffrey! You should be ashamed of that shot.'

Geoffrey merely grinned. Roz had gone to fetch the ball. She tossed it to Barry. He walked up to Di but kept the ball behind his back.

'Time out, Di love. Roz has an important question.'

Di frowned but recognised Barry's non-messing tone. She gave Roz a thin, patient smile.

'Can Lenny come to my party at the club on Saturday? It's after the match,' asked Roz.

'What time will stumps be pulled on this party?'

'Nine at the latest,' said Roz.

Di closed her eyes and made a meal of pondering. 'If it had been a Friday night, before a game, I'd have said no. But . . .' Di opened her eyes and grinned savagely. 'But as we are going to grind Ransons Sports into the daisies, it's fine by me.'

'Oh thanks,' gasped Roz. She and Zoë began to trot towards the french windows.

'Stay a bit and join in,' said Di.

'No,' said Barry. 'They're off to Sloggers to practise.'

Di turned back to the cricket and Barry saw the girls back to the hall.

After picking up her gear and the envelopes Roz looked beseechingly at Barry. 'Er, Mr Higgs, I hope you don't think this is cheeky, but I really came round in person to see you about a special favour.'

'I know,' said Barry, 'you want my recipe for garlic sausage rolls.'

Roz laughed. 'No, but close. I wonder, could you do a buffet for my party? You don't have to go as way out as you did . . .'

Barry looked like a wizard who had just learned a new spell. 'Say no more. I will prepare a mixture of the solid and the sublime – how's about curried shrimps, sweet and sour barm cakes, pasta shells with mushy peas, black pudding with honey . . .'

'Fine, fine.' Roz held up her hands in surrender.

'One last condition.' Barry's eyes narrowed in comic malice. 'I insist that Pat Masters be invited so I can show her the rest of my culinary curiosities.'

'Done,' said Roz. The girls swung off happily for the practice.

It was ten minutes to twelve before a very thoughtful Lenny met Donna on the seat at the town end of Green Lane. Donna had changed into her track suit and was sitting happily holding a tin of Uncle Joe's Mint Balls. She offered the tin to Lenny. He took a sweet and began to suck it pensively.

'You look like a wet weekend in Wigan, Lenny Higgs.' Donna dug him hard in the ribs. 'The team needs bounce, character, enthusiasm today. What's up with yer?'

Lenny sighed. 'I've just had a sort of heart-to-heart with Dot. She's furious that my mum is so against my fiddling. There should be time for Viv Richards and Vivaldi, she says. And there's a Lancashire Youth Orchestra starting soon. She reckons I could get in – *if* I practise hard.'

'Well, we'll just have to make sure you do. At Dot's, round mine, in the score-box, in a cow shed up on the moors.' Donna was gushing. She started to sing, rattling the tin of sweets in tune.

> 'Uncle Joe's, Joe's Mint Balls,
> Are the best you'll ever know.'

Lenny grinned and joined in.

> 'Give them to your granny,
> And watch your granny go.'

Lenny put his arm around Donna's shoulders and they were swaying from side to side like fans on the Kop.

Round the bend Roz and Zoë stopped when they heard the singing. Roz frowned and peered round the bushes. She froze.

'What's up?' asked Zoë.

'Donna – rotten – Rothwell is sitting on a seat brazen as brass, trying to pinch my bloke.' Roz took out the invitation marked 'Donna'. She tore it to shreds and chucked it into the beck. 'No way is she coming to my party.'

Before Zoë could speak Roz was stalking towards the seat. Eyes sparkling with fun, Donna offered the tin of sweets.

'Keep your stupid sweets, pal, I can buy my own.' Roz spat the words out.

Donna turned red and Lenny stood up. 'Who rattled your cage, Crabtree?' he asked stonily.

Roz clutched the invitation, sneered at Donna and looked strictly at Lenny. 'I'm having a party for my *friends*,' said Roz. 'On Saturday in the clubhouse. Will you be coming?'

Lenny looked from Roz to the crestfallen Donna and back. 'Is Donna invited?'

'As a matter of fact – no.'

Lenny picked up his coffin and took Donna by the arm. 'Then you can count me out as well, pal.' They moved off towards the Sloggers' ground.

Roz shrieked after them. 'But there's going to be a "Do Your Own Thing" cabaret. You can play your fiddle, Lenny. And your dad's doing the buffet. Sweet and sour barm cakes...'

Neither Donna nor Lenny turned round.

'Nice one, Roz,' sighed Zoë.

The cricket practice was not a success. Neither Donna nor Lenny turned up. This upset Stan so he was extra hard on errors; so the team made more. After forty-five minutes Stan called enough, and everybody drifted into the clubhouse. Jason and Malcolm began playing pool with 100 per cent more enthusiasm than they had summoned earlier for cricket.

Malcolm fluked a red into the middle bag.

'Awesome,' said Jason.

'Welles,' replied Malcolm. He began to chalk his cue casually. 'He were a famous film star, weren't he, Stan?'

'Who?' asked Stan turning from the window.

'Awesome Welles.'

'Funnee,' said Stan. It was obvious that he was doing his best to keep his feelings bottled up. Stan walked past the pool table to where Roz, wearing a bright smile, was standing by Scooby.

'Do you know where Lenny is?' Stan asked Roz awkwardly. Before she could reply, a funny ringing noise began in Scooby's holdall. He pulled out his mum's posaphone.

'Thanks for the enquiry about my bat-making,' said Scooby almost rudely into the phone. 'But remember these bats are hand-made by a craftsman.' For the benefit of his audience he pointed to himself. 'I want thirty-five. Right. Ten now, and five pounds a week. You won't regret it, sir.' He put the phone away and addressed the room. 'Told you my bat-making business would make me a fortune.'

'How many orders you got?' asked Slasher.

'Just the one,' admitted Scooby. 'But it's a start. I'll bet Mr Mini started off his car business with just the one.'

A couple of jeers were stifled as Stan at last erupted. 'What with you doing a Richard Branson,' he glared at Scooby, 'and Lenny knocking, and the rest of you practising like a set of puff-balls, I don't know why I bother.'

The venom did not dilute Scooby's cool. 'I expect our Leonard is having a spot of private coaching under the beady eye of you-know-who.'

'Or his dad's teaching him to make garlic shepherd's pie,' said Bugle. 'First, take one shepherd...'

'Or the lad's out on the fiddle,' said Bal miming playing a violin.

There was no fun in Roz's crack. 'Or he's down the end of Green Lane making google-eyes at our dear scorer.'

Zoë glared at Roz. Stan shrugged deeply and went back to stare at the pitch. Roz reckoned it was time to lift the gloom. She pulled the invitations from her cricket bag. Everyone but Stan crowded round. Roz held up her head for hush. 'Saturday is my fourteenth birthday and I'm having a special party here after the match.'

'A rave?' asked Jason, eyes flaring.

'No. Better,' said Roz. 'You're all invited.' The kids passed round the invites and took their own. 'You'll see it mentions a cabaret. Well, it's a "Do Your Own Thing" party and I don't want any presents. All I want is six volunteers to each do a turn.'

Matey looked suspicious. 'What kind of turn?'

'For example,' Roz pointed to Zoë with an evil grin, 'Zoë here has promised to do a spot of ballet.'

Zoë's look of amazement showed that it was news to her.

Malcolm put his hand up. 'If you promise not to call me a poser – all of you – I'll show my physique – to music.' To cries of approval he pulled off his shirt and did an 'audition'.

'Right,' laughed Roz. 'You're in.'

Matey was standing with Bal. He coughed loudly and everybody looked at him. He went pink. 'I can do a turn, Roz, I think. Put me down for "Albert and the Lion".' Bal shook his head in an ominous fashion but said nowt.

Scooby was languidly checking his diary. 'If I'm not too busy, I'll act as MC,' Scooby drawled.

'Gee thanks, Lord Muck,' said Roz.

Stan could never keep a monk on long with the Sloggers' lot. During the chat about turns he had moved close to Roz. Roz handed him an invite. 'Lenny could do a bit on his violin,' suggested Stan. 'If he can be bothered to turn up.'

Roz's look showed that she was not keen on the idea, but nobody asked her why. Suddenly Jason turned from the pool table holding three of the balls. 'Right. On

Saturday the Great Jaceamundo will demonstrate the art of juggling.' He hurled the balls aloft, caught one, and the other two fell to the floor, one banging his knee.

'Don't call us,' said Roz.

The idea had certainly caught on. Jason retired to a corner for more practice. Malcolm was doing press-ups to work on his muscles. Zoë was flexing her legs and chucking in the odd pirouette. And Matey had Bal in a corner listening to his tale of a boy-eating lion in Blackpool.

'Wish I could get them half as keen on cricket, lass,' said Stan to Roz. 'Right, you lot, gather round, calm down and let's discuss the whole matter of beating Ransons Sports on Saturday.' As Stan spoke a grim-faced Lenny walked in, stared everybody out and sat down by the window. Stan noticed the hostile looks Lenny was giving Roz but he stuck to the team talk. 'Against Ransons, I'll remind you all, it's a twenty-over game. We need responsible batting,' here Stan gave a withering look at Slasher, 'but no stonewalling for averages. We must balance caution with aggression.'

'Stan.' Matey had his hand up and an expression of pure innocence in his eye. 'Is it an old Lancashire proverb, "balance caution with aggression"?'

'No,' flashed Stan. 'It's a Country and Western song.'

Minds were still on the party pieces. Jason was trying to balance a piece of blue pool chalk on his nose. Stan ignored this and waded on. 'So let's use our noddles on Saturday. Lenny, owt to add?'

Lenny's voice was tight, his face pale, and he never took his eyes off Roz. 'Me and Donna missed the practice for personal reasons.' Nobody was thinking about the party now. Roz glared back at Lenny. He went on. 'Against Dobby we all chipped in, on the field and in the tea-room.' Nobody was laughing or joking now. 'I want us to play like a team against Ransons.' Again he stared pointedly at Roz. 'In cricket you can't just do your own thing.' With that he stalked out.

Malcolm voiced what several were thinking. 'Lenny's mum must be giving him stick again.'

Zoë looked hard at Roz and shook her head sadly. Roz brazened on. 'Party starts at six-thirty. Mr Barry Higgs is providing an ace buffet.'

This brightened things up. Bal looked deep in thought, but not for long. Matey dragged him into a corner. 'Right. 'Ere we go,' said Matey. 'There's a famous – er – place – er – by the sea – er – known as . . .'

'Blackpool,' said Bal.

'Yes,' said Matey in triumph. 'That is noted for – for – for . . .'

'Candy floss. Battered cod and chips. You *have* got a job on, Matey.'

As so often when Di was out of the way there was a calm glow abroad in the Higgses' lounge. Lenny was still seething about Roz's behaviour and the effect it had had on Donna. Both had been too upset to attend the practice. If I'd gone I'd have given Roz Crabtree a right mouthful, thought Lenny. One day the team's going to need Donna . . . Lenny hid his thoughts behind the evening paper.

Barry Higgs's mood was the total opposite of his son's. He was sitting at the table across the room making notes on a pile of papers. On his face was the hopeful smile of a wizard trying to make gold out of lead. He snapped his fingers and chucked down his pencil. 'I think I've got it, our Len.' Lenny looked over the top of the paper. 'What do you reckon to chicken legs done in a hickory sauce with just a smidgen of Mexican pepper? What do you think of that for Roz's buffet?'

Lenny tried to be politely enthusiastic but it came out dead flat. 'Dad, if you plonked down chicken with HP sauce, and a dash of Branston, the team would think it was a banquet.'

Barry frowned. 'If you don't mind me saying, you seem less than wild about this do.'

'I'm not going to the do, Dad.' Lenny did not look up over the paper.

Barry walked slowly across the room. He took the *Dobcroft Herald* from Lenny. 'What about my gourmet buffet?' Barry spoke softly then his tone turned cheeky. 'What about your party piece?' Lenny sat upright in shock. 'What about a touch of the Nigel Kennedy's on the old school fiddle?'

'What – er – fiddle?' asked Lenny lamely.

Barry shushed him with a wide grin. 'The other day when your mum was out, thank heavens, our Geoffrey went snooping in your coffin and dragged it out. He was trying to hit an onion for six with it when I caught him.' Barry pointed to the ceiling. 'Don't worry, her upstairs is none the wiser.'

'Thanks, Dad,' Lenny sighed. 'Mrs Ball says I've got to keep at it. They're starting a Lancashire Youth Orchestra soon, and she reckons I would get in.'

Barry struggled to keep his laugh in. 'That's all we need. Imagine your mum's face if she found out that cricket for Yorkshire was playing second fiddle to music for Lancashire.'

They both laughed. Then Lenny came over serious again. 'I'm dead keen on my music.' Once more he refused to make eye contact.

'Look, our kid, *I'm* dead keen on your being happy.' Barry sat on the edge of the chair. 'How is it you're not going to the party?'

At last there was a bit of life in Lenny's voice. 'Well, you know what women are like.' Barry slowly raised his eyes to the ceiling. Di's footsteps could be heard banging around in the bedroom. Lenny continued, 'Well, Roz fancies me rotten. But she thinks Donna fancies me too.'

'Mr Drop-Dead Gorgeous, is it?' Barry joked.

'Roz saw me and Donna larking about in Green Lane and she went ape. Said Donna couldn't come to the party. So I told her to scratch me as well.'

'You did dead right there, our kid,' said Barry. Then a

small frown wrinkled his brow. 'You're sure you and Donna are just pals and no more?'

Lenny pursed his lips in frustration. 'Dad! I'm your son. I'm not the last of the red-hot lover boys.'

Barry threw up his hands in a pantomime of shame-horror. There was the muffled sound of footsteps on the landing upstairs. Di's voice echoed softly. 'Night, night, sleep tight.' Geoffrey's giggly little voice responded. 'Ni-ni-eep-ti,' followed by a thud as Wisden was chucked off his bed. Barry immersed himself in his menu notes. Lenny half wrapped himself in the *Dobcroft Herald*.

Di bounced into the room. 'How are the team, Lenny?' She was disgustingly enthusiastic. 'Together in their heads? Minds fixed on Saturday's match?'

Lenny replied like a pre-recorded message. 'Thank you for calling – the team, all the lot of them, are one hundred per cent dedicated. No external interests.' He pantomimed the last words. 'Ha-rotten-ha-rotten-ha.' There was a ghost of a chuckle from Barry.

FOUR

The following Saturday was not at all an ideal day for cricket. By 12.30 there had been several heavy showers of rain. But certain people in the Sloggers' team did not mind about the rain; they were seriously focused on other things.

'Take me through it again?' whined Matey to Bal. With a sigh Bal opened the book and like a runner starting a marathon off went Matey. 'There's a seaside place called Blackpool...'

These two were part of what looked like a troupe of strolling players practising their 'turns' under an oak tree at Ransons' Sports Ground. Zoë was in her cricket whites but was doing the odd *plié*, her face a mask of concentration. Jason was juggling after a fashion with two tatty batting gloves and a helmet. Malcolm, in muscle vest, flexed his pecs and lats. 'Ooh,' he screeched as Jason's helmet hit a branch of the tree and brought a shower of icy droplets down on to his bare skin.

'Sorry,' hissed Jason.

Lenny walked up to them with his cricket coffin and a don't-call-us-we'll-call-you look on his face. 'Right, *luvvies*. If you lot can stop thesping for a mo', I'll remind you that in half an hour we are due to *perform* with bat and ball. So – knock it on the head, huh?'

The strolling players got the message and picked up their cricket gear – all except Matey who kept on burbling. Lenny reached into Matey's cricket bag and pulled out the fines book.

'I'm fining all of you ten pence for bad attitude,' said Lenny, only half serious. 'But you,' he pointed to Matey, 'I'm fining you twenty.'

Lenny scrawled in the book.

Matey stopped declaiming and stuck out a pet-lip at Lenny. 'Why an extra ten pence for me?'

'Because of the situation in Timbuktu, that's why,' rapped Lenny.

'But I don't even know where it is,' complained Matey.

'Well, you should do!' Lenny pointed to the pavilion. They all grumbled off.

Donna walked past the tree, not noticing Lenny under the lower branches. She was, as usual, looking very smart, and had applied the faintest dab of make-up. She had the Sloggers' scorebook under one arm, and was holding a carrier bag.

'Is that your lunch?' joked Lenny.

Donna turned, saw him and joined him under the tree. Her brief grin vanished and she spoke quietly. 'I've been doing a bit of thinking, Lenny, and I reckon you should go to the party because you're the captain. It'll only make the atmosphere more sour if you don't go. And your dad will expect you there.'

Lenny took a while to reply. She had obviously thought this through. It was typical of Donna that she was looking to patch up a row caused by others. Lenny chucked her under the chin. There was no grin. 'I'm not going to the do,' he said firmly and softly. 'Just think, girl, while that lot are prancing and posing we can go fiddling in the old bandstand in the park.'

As if on cue, Dot Ball joined them. She took down her brolly and peered out at the dying shower. 'Damp, but I reckon we'll play.' She turned to Donna. 'OK if I join you in the score-box, my dear?'

'Sure,' said Donna.

'Are you getting plenty of *practice*?' Dot looked sternly at Lenny

'Here and there – mostly there,' Lenny said.

He was glad to see Donna drag Dot away to avoid any further grilling on his efforts with the fiddle. One day my life will be simple, Lenny thought whimsically. He ran across to the pavilion as his mother entered the ground with Geoffrey. She was holding an enormous blue and yellow Yorkshire County Cricket Club umbrella. She took up position outside the pavilion. An unwitting Stan Topping almost collided with her as he bustled round the corner of the pavilion.

'Hey up,' said Di by way of greeting.

Stan pushed his flat cap back on his head and looked at Di warily. 'How are you today, Mrs Higgs?'

'I'm fine,' rapped Di. 'We'll be lucky to get a full game in today.' Di took down the brolly. The rain had stopped. She continued, 'Late start, I reckon, then a ten-over thrash.' She turned her gaze from Stan to the cover over the wicket. 'If *I* was team supremo, I wouldn't be out here looking at the weather. I'd be in with the team sorting things out. Discussing options.'

Stan bristled. 'My team *know* all the options.'

Di leapt in like a flash. 'Oh, they do, do they. Well, what bright spark decided on last week's crazy batting order? Strange options there.'

Stan licked his lips for maximum retort. 'Leonard Henry Higgs decided the order – off his own bat.' Stan twigged the unintentional pun but bottled his mirth. He continued, 'And may I remind you that we won.'

Di went down like a balloon landing on a hedgehog. 'So what's the plan right now?' she asked softly.

Stan pulled his cap forward in a business-like fashion. 'I have my own plan for keeping the team alert during any delay.' Airy-fairy as you like, he added, 'Drop into the changing room in a tick. You might learn summat.'

Lancashire 1, Yorkshire 0, thought Stan.

A delay in starting of at least one hour had been announced. So Stan's wheeze for keeping the Sloggers team alert was in operation. It was a cricket quiz and Stan acted as the question-master. Some of the team were showing more alertness than others.

Jason was hovering near the door clutching three cricket balls. He was twitching to get in some juggling practice. Scooby sat near the back with his mum's po-saphone under a towel. He was expecting an important call. In the front row Bugle, ever a widehead, looked eager. So did Matey who was clutching his fines book.

'OK, easy question,' said Stan. 'Who, in cricket, is known as "Beefy"?'

'Arnold Schwarzenegger,' offered Malcolm, flexing his pecs.

'That'll be a ten-pence fine for flippancy,' rasped Stan.

'And I'll pay ten pence if Malcolm can spell it,' said Bugle.

Stan looked straight at Slasher. 'Who is "Beefy"?'

'Ian Botham,' said Slasher.

'Right,' said Stan. 'Now...'

Scooby's posaphone began to ring. Scooby answered it as though he was in the boardroom of ICI. 'Timothy Masters here.' He listened intently for a few seconds. 'If they move above a hundred and sixty – buy!' He scrambled the phone away and stared Stan down. 'My broker,' he explained.

There was a sudden gasp from Roz who was looking out of the window. 'Oh-oh. Severe depression heading in this direction – from Yorkshire,' Roz laughed.

Lenny shot her a dagger glance. Di came in quietly and stood by the door. Jason slipped out.

'Next question,' said Stan. 'True or false? Overarm bowling was first used by a woman.'

The 'humph' of disapproval from Di could have been heard in Rochdale. 'Everyone knows that is TRUE,' sneered Di. 'The question is far too easy. Now if I were manager...'

Most of the kids groaned. Lenny wanted to hide under a stone. Why could his mum never keep her mouth shut?

'You are not the manager, Mrs H. I asked you in here to observe, not to stage a takeover bid.'

Di haughtily moved to the window. Stan went on, 'Next question...'

'Er – Mr Manager,' crowed Di, 'if this quiz is supposed to keep the team on their toes,' she pointed out of the window, 'what is Jason doing out there?'

There was a rush to the window, by everyone except Stan. Jason was juggling the three cricket balls furiously. He was facing the window. When he saw he had an audience he began to show off. 'You ain't seen nothing yet, folks.'

He hurled all three balls high in the air. He caught the first two down, took off his baseball cap and tried to catch the last ball in it. The ball hit him right between the eyes. He dropped like a stone.

Nobody laughed. Nobody said a dicky-bird. Except Di. 'What are your options now?' she asked Stan icily. Scooby led a small posse off to take care of Jason.

'I'll take the idiot to Casualty,' said Stan to Lenny. 'You go and fetch Donna.'

'Donna,' screeched Di. 'I'm not sure about that.'

'Nor me,' said Roz loudly.

'Well, I am,' said Lenny. 'Bring juggling Jace into the changing room and take off his gear. Donna will have to wear it.'

Lenny and Stan left the room. Di looked out of the window at Jason who was still horizontal but groaning loudly. 'Options,' she hissed to herself. 'Panic stations more like.'

A quarter of an hour later Sloggers' openers, Roz and Scooby, went out to bat. Ransons had won the toss and put Sloggers in. The game was reduced to a ten-over thrash. Orders had been given to whack the bad balls, and Scooby had hit two fours in the first over. Roz prodded back the first two balls of the second over.

Lenny was not pleased. He stood up from the bench he was sharing with Donna. 'Hit out or get out, Roz,' he yelled.

Roz glared at him and stuck her tongue out. She lashed the next ball for four.

'Psychology, see,' said Lenny to Donna.

She did not answer. Jason's cricket shirt and trousers were miles too big for her. And she felt a prize divvy in his white baseball cap. 'Do I have to wear this monstrosity?' she asked Lenny, taking the hat off.

'No,' he laughed.

She hurled the cap inside their dressing-room window. 'I hope I haven't got to bat,' she muttered.

'You'll be reet,' said Lenny. 'It's not you I'm worried about.' He gave meaningful glances at Zoë, Matey and Malcolm.

In the score-box Dot Ball had taken over from Donna. She was now joined by Di, with notebook and binoculars. Dot was also acting as minder to Geoffrey Higgs.

Di surveyed the batting. 'Go for your shots, you two. Give 'em some pasty!' Her voice could have stripped paint. She turned to Dot. 'I don't mind telling you, Mrs Ball, that I'm very concerned about the application of this team. Stan runs a very slack ship.'

Dot grinned back. 'On the contrary, the side seems shipshape and Bristol fashion to me.'

Before Di could reply Bal and Matey came wandering round the boundary. They stopped in front of Di, and Bal held up the 'Albert and the Lion' text. Matey put his right hand on his heart and gave it his all.

'Now Albert had heard about – er...'

'Lions,' said Bal with a shake of his head.

'Yes – lions,' said Matey. 'How they were anti-social like...'

'Ferocious and wild!' Bal was losing patience now. 'I reckon you should forget this and do some impressions at the party.'

'Party,' Di screamed. She grabbed the book from Bal and stuck it in her shopping bag. 'Get your minds on this game, you gobslotches.'

Bal and Matey ran off.

In the middle Scooby cracked an elegant four to take the score to 18 for 0. As the fielders scrabbled in the long grass looking for the ball, Scooby ambled down the wicket to Roz. 'I've been thinking, our kid.' Scooby batted a divot down with his bat. 'I *will* probably do the MC-ing for your cabaret. I thought a bow tie and straw hat might be appropriate.'

Roz strove to keep her cool. 'Thanks – but right now I wish you'd keep your mind on the game!'

Scooby shrugged, sauntered back to the crease and held the bat like a baseball hitter. He swung lazily at the ball, got a top edge and was easily caught by the wicket-keeper. Roz shook her head.

'Plenty of time to rehearse my ad libs,' said Scooby as he passed her.

Lenny walked to the crease with a grim face. 'Play your shots, our Leonard,' his mother yelped. I could do without that, he thought. Roz would not look him straight in the eyes. Ransons Sports' fielders sensed the unease in the Sloggers team. They crowded the bat. Lenny had the feeling that if he failed, the team would fail. But in a ten-over thrash you had to chance your arm. He hit the first two balls for four.

It was too good to last. Lenny tried to hook a ball, played early and was caught. There was not a peep from the Sloggers contingent as Lenny marched swiftly from the pitch. Bugle strode to the wicket flashing his bat like a broadsword. Lenny sat down between Zoë and Donna who were both padded up.

'That was a rubbish shot,' Lenny said to Donna. She nodded. 'So don't play it when you go in. You're next.' Donna flinched but said nothing. Lenny went on: 'Keep one end tight and tell Roz to go for it.'

'Howzat!' came the cry from the middle as Bugle's wild swipe missed the ball and the timber toppled. Donna stood up. She took Lenny's bat and set off to the middle.

At the score-box, Di turned to Dot. 'It's a mistake to send this lass in now. No experience.'

'But plenty upstairs, Mrs Higgs,' Dot retorted. 'Come on, Donna,' she yelled.

Roz was waiting for Donna in the middle with a

wary, hostile look on her face. Donna refused to be fazed. 'Lenny says that I have to block, and you have to have a bash.' Donna said it loud and clear, not caring if the Ransons' lot heard or not.

Roz turned away snootily. 'Just try not to get out, *dearie*,' was her cheap crack.

Donna bit her lip and kept in a riposte.

'You two girls out here to bat or chinwag?' asked the Ransons' skipper.

Donna prodded the remaining balls of the over back to the bowler. There were heavy sighs and snorts of derision from the fielders. Donna ignored them.

Roz went to town. She flayed the bowling to all parts of the field and after nine overs Sloggers had scored 56 for 3. Lenny stood in the middle of the team who were all cheering the girls on. 'Sssh,' said Lenny. In the hush his lone voice echoed out. 'Right, lasses. Last over. Give it big licks.'

Matey and Bugle began to chant. 'Big licks. Big licks!'

Roz steered the first ball to square leg. 'Running,' she screamed and set off.

Donna spotted a fielder racing in and yelled, 'No.' Roz continued. The ball was flung hard to the wicket-keeper. Roz and Donna were almost nose to nose at Donna's end. The 'keeper whipped off the bails. Donna stepped almost elegantly out of the crease. She was out.

'Thanks,' whispered Roz.

'It's for the good of the team, *dearie*,' said Donna. The Sloggers' lot cheered her to the echo.

'Sorry, skip,' she said to Lenny.

'You did the right thing,' said Lenny. 'Roz's fault. Never a run there. She'd better give it some welly now.'

With Zoë at the other end, Roz crashed two fours and a two. Sloggers finished with sixty-six.

'It might just be enough,' said Lenny as they clapped off Zoë and Roz.

Fifteen minutes later the Sloggers' team were fielding and they were not happy.

Ransons' openers had obviously decided to play safe and steady for the first few overs then have a bash. Big black clouds filled the sky as Slasher came in to bowl the fourth over. Ransons had scored only three runs. The Ransons' skipper poised to hoik the ball, lost his bottle and dead-batted it. Slasher gave a theatrical yawn. Bugle coughed loudly. The skipper turned. ''Ere, mate, riddle for yer. What's red, made of leather, and *can* be hit off the square?'

As Slasher ran in to bowl, the heavens opened, the umpire grabbed the bails and everybody ran off the pitch. The rain really set in for the rest of the day and at 3.30 it was announced that play was over. Sloggers were the winners on faster-run rate.

'So it's a good job that I crashed them early on,' bragged Scooby.

Everybody groaned. Stan held up his hands for order. 'I'd just like to say that Juggling Jason is OK. He'll be at the party later. And I want to add my thanks today to Donna. She was put on the spot but did the business magnificently.'

Everyone in the dressing room applauded, especially Roz. 'I was a right wally today,' she said. This was greeted with cries of assent. 'And I was a wally over my party. Donna, I'd like you to come tonight.'

For a couple of ticks there was an awkward silence. Donna seemed to be weighing her words. 'Well – I think,' she paused, 'I think I will.'

There were more cheers. 'But only,' said Donna, 'if I can do a turn.'

'Violin?' asked Roz.

'Wait and see.' Donna tapped her nose.

Matey waved the fines book. 'Right, Roz. I am fining you ten pence.'

'Why?' Roz laughed. 'For being a wally?'

'No, for mentioning a party in the club dressing room on a match day.'

*

At around five o'clock that evening Barry was trying to put the finishing touches to his exotic buffet, but he was having trouble. As he fluttered round his creations adding a sprig of parsley here and a few peppers there, he was bombarded with details of the victory from Di and Dot Ball. They had burst into Sloggers' clubhouse ten minutes earlier with little Geoffrey and they'd done nothing but yak.

Dot held the scorebook as though it was a battle standard. 'We got eighteen runs off the first three overs...'

'Scooby's slogging,' snorted Di.

Dot frowned. 'Risky, I admit, but in their first three overs Ransons only scored three runs. I'll remind you, Mrs Higgs, that we won.'

'We?' queried Di.

'We!' said Dot clutching the scorebook possessively. Dot obviously now considered herself a full member of the club.

Barry leapt in to save a scene. 'So *we* will all be in high spirits for the party tonight,' he said brightly.

Di sighed. 'I wish I could be there tonight to see some of these turns. Matey's going to spout poetry and I think Jason's going to juggle despite his injury.'

Barry looked up at the roof. Thank goodness she's going to be nowhere near this room tonight, he thought.

'If we had thought on we could have got a babysitter,' said Di. ''Bye.'

As the door clicked to, Barry turned to Dot. 'So Donna didn't let the side down, did she?'

'She certainly didn't.' Dot's eyes glowed.

Two hours later Lenny Higgs looked around the merry throng filling the clubhouse and pulled his violin case from his coffin. He was a bit nervous about performing in public, but it was a night for enthusiasm rather than excellence. His dad's buffet had been a roaring success and there was not a scrap left. Now Barry was manning the tape deck and the 'turns' were getting ready.

Jason was wandering round with the Wally of the Day jester's cap on and showing off the bump on his forehead and two black eyes.

Matey was wearing an old brown pin-striped suit and a bowler hat. Zoë had gone off to change into ballet gear, and Malcolm was looking cool in a silver lurex muscle vest.

Most fuss had been caused by Donna's outfit. She was wearing a long cape, blue trimmed with white. But she refused to give any hint about her act.

A pile of presents littered the top of the pool table, and Lenny joined Roz as she started opening them. Scooby, in bow tie and straw hat, was with Roz. 'Right, skip, I thought I'd introduce you as Slogthwaite's answer to Nigel Kennedy. OK?' asked Scooby.

'Say what you like, pal.' Lenny smiled.

Donna walked across the room with a carrier bag. She pulled out a parcel and gave it to Roz. 'Happy birthday,' said Donna.

Lenny noticed the colour rise in Roz's cheeks. 'Thanks,' said Roz meekly.

Scooby was digging under the pile of presents. ''Ere, what's this?' He lifted a tatty brown-paper parcel. He read the writing scrawled on it. 'To Roz and all the team.' There was a silence as the kids crowded round. Roz unwrapped the paper. She lifted the lid of a flat box. Inside were a dozen pork pies.

'The Pie Piper strikes again,' said Scooby.

'Who can he be?' asked Roz.

'More important, are his wares up to scratch?' asked Bugle grabbing a pie. Slasher and Malcolm followed suit.

'Don't be daft. We've just finished my dad's buffet,' Lenny shouted and lifted the box of pies high above his head. 'We'll share these out *after* the cabaret.'

'Good thinking, skip,' said Scooby. He raised his voice. 'Right, ladies and gentlemen, please take your seats because it's show time.'

The first act got the crowd really going. Jason had been persuaded to abandon cricket balls and use tennis balls in his performance. After three minutes of juggling without dropping a ball, Jason climaxed his act by *heading* all three balls into the audience. There was loud applause as he walked off.

'Thanks, folks.' Scooby was in his element as MC. 'Now for our first bit of culture. A bit of bobby-dazzling ballet from Miss Zoë Milner.'

By the light of a reading lamp Di Higgs was making notes in a school exercise book. In a sombre voice she read back what she had written. 'Sloggers' log. Generally, the team have an attitude problem. Their minds are allowed to wander. They get their sloppy heads on. We urgently need a manager who is dedicated, firm, single-minded and not afraid to dish out short, sharp shocks...'

Her concentration was broken by the phone ringing. It was Dot Ball. She was offering to do Di a favour.

'I know how much you'd like to see the kids do their party pieces,' said Dot. 'So I'll pop round and babysit Geoffrey for you.'

Di grinned. 'All right. It's very kind of you. Geoffrey's been off like a top for a good hour now. It'll take me ten minutes to get decent.' She looked down at her track suit. 'See you in a bit, and thanks again, Dot.'

The cabaret was proving to be a roaring success. Polite applause for Zoë's ballet piece was replaced by jeers, cheers and finally roars of approval for 'Albert and the Lion'. Matey made such a mess of the words that Bal had to get up and finish the performance (Bal was word perfect) while Matey pathetically mimed words and actions.

Malcolm's musical muscles kept the pot boiling, then it was Donna's turn to raise a few eyebrows. Still wearing her cape she mounted the stage carrying two mysterious bits of wood. The tape started, Donna took off the cape to reveal a majorette's outfit, and she began to baton-twirl.

Jason looked on in envy and the whole side began to clap in time with the music. The applause at the end was deafening.

''Ere, I reckon we should incorporate that into our next fielding practice,' said Stan.

'Good idea,' said Lenny as a flutter of nerves winged through his stomach.

Scooby was carefully arranging a chair in the middle of the stage. The lights went down in the rest of the room. Scooby picked up the microphone and became very solemn. 'Now, pin back your lug'oles for a bit of culture. Our next turn is ace with a cricket bat and with a fiddle. Put your hands together for Lenny Higgs.'

There was generous applause as Lenny walked on to the stage, sat down, closed his eyes and began to tune up. Nobody noticed Di slip in the door. She froze. Lenny stopped tuning up and paused before beginning. There was a clack of shoes on the wooden floor. Faces turned. It was not a pretty sight.

Di's face was like a gargoyle on an ancient church. People began to whisper. As Lenny began to play, eyes still shut, Di walked on the stage and gently trapped his bow-arm.

Everybody could hear Di's words. ''Appen you've been spending too much time with that, and not enough with your bat, my lad.' She took the violin from Lenny. There were angry voices from the crowd. Lenny walked off.

'That's quite enough, dear,' said Barry icily.

Di burst into tears and rushed from the room, leaving the fiddle on the chair. Barry put a loud disco number on the tape deck. 'Boogie time,' he yelled.

In relief several people started to dance.

FIVE

Next morning, Sunday, Lenny sat in his bedroom as his parents had a 'discussion' over breakfast. Despite the sound of his mother's voice raised in anguish and anger, Lenny could not keep a grin from spreading over his chops. OK, she is a pain. OK, she shows me up from time to time, he thought. But, thanks to my dad, we have ways of dealing with her. There was about to be a charade to keep his mum sweet.

'Lenny,' his dad's voice rang out. 'Can you come down here a minute?'

Lenny wiped the grin away, and, face as long as a fiddle, walked slowly downstairs. In the kitchen Barry stood with a face of stone, and Di sat rubbing tears from her eyes.

'Your mother has a few words to say about her performance at Sloggers last night,' Barry said through tight lips.

Lenny put on the face of a Christian about to face a dozen hungry lions in a Roman arena. Don't laugh, he nagged himself.

Di snuffled and began her speech very quietly. 'I want to apologise, Leonard, for putting the mockers on your do last night.' Lenny knew his mum would not stay at force five for long. 'But you conned me. You have been hiding that rotten fiddle in your coffin.' Rising force seven, Lenny thought. 'Once you were totally dedicated to cricket. Like Geoffrey Boycott himself you ate, slept and drank batting. But now there's a worm in the apple...'

Barry raised his eyes to the kitchen ceiling. Lenny could feel a giggle rising. He turned it into a sneeze.

'Exactly,' Barry almost shouted. 'That fiddle is banned from this house, young man. Go get your coffin.'

Still wearing the hangdog expression Lenny went into the hall and came back with the coffin.

'Take the fiddle out and give it here.' Barry's acting of the heartless villain part was so bad it would have got him chucked out of the Slogthwaite Players, but it worked a treat on Di.

With a flounce Lenny opened the lid and chucked out all his cricket gear – bats, pads, whites, socks, boots, gloves, the lot. There was no sign of the violin case.

The gale had blown itself out. Di began to weep gently. It was time for Lenny's big scene. 'I knew the fiddle had to go, Mum, so it's gone.'

Di clutched him to her bosom. 'Thank you, son, thank you,' she sniffled between sobs.

Over her shoulder Barry gave Lenny a big wink. If only she knew where the fiddle had gone to ...

At 6 p.m. the following Wednesday an unusual form of fielding practice was in full swing at Sloggers' ground. For some reason Stan was late, so Lenny had got the kids all going at baton-twirling. Donna had brought along the batons. As usual, some were more serious about practice than others.

Lenny's group and Roz's group were doing their best to twirl and toss the batons to each other. It certainly did give the fingers a work-out. But Jason, Bugle, Craig and Matey, in a group of their own, were looking daft. They were merely trying to toss the baton as high as possible. Their shrieks of merriment could be heard right down the end of Green Lane.

'Pack it in, you lot,' shouted Lenny. 'Stan will do 'is pieces if he catches you mucking about.'

Jason and Co took no notice. Roz had a go at them. 'Look, be serious, we've got the Cup Match against Sandwell on Sunday. So please be serious.'

It was no good. Jason hurled the baton to a ridiculous height. 'Catch it!' he shouted as Di paraded into the ground ahead of Barry and Geoffrey.

'Someone's gonna catch it,' said Matey.

Di caught the baton and breezed over to Roz who was holding another one. She tugged it from her hands. Donna looked away in embarrassment. Lenny held on to his group's baton. His mother had more sense than to try and pull it away from him.

'Give me that silly stick,' said Di.

Lenny glared at her. 'It's not a stick. And there is no way this is silly. Stan saw Donna's act at the party and said it would help our fielding.'

This obviously took a bit of the wind out of Di's sails. She handed Lenny the two batons. 'Fair dos. But there was some messing about going on,' she glowered at Jason, 'you can't deny that.' A crafty grin slid across her face. 'And if Stan Topping's so keen on novel training methods, why is he not here to supervise them? Surely he knows it's the Cup on Sunday.'

Roz was quick to Stan's defence. 'Stan has a rotten cold. I saw him at tea-time coming out of the chemist's. He looked like death.'

Di's grin flowered. 'Oh, in that case *I* will take the practice.'

The jolly mood of the practice evaporated. There were muted groans. Why doesn't Stan turn up and take charge? wondered Lenny. Who knows what my mother has in mind.

'Running,' Di stated. 'Off you all go. Four laps of the field. Last one past the score-box each lap is fined ten pence.'

The team trotted off. Di led Barry and Geoffrey off towards the score-box.

'Are you sure long-distance running is good for junior cricketers, dear?' asked Barry gently. 'Surely practising the tactics would be a better idea.'

'Faster, faster. Pump them arms. Get your knees up,' Di hollered, a manic gleam in her eye. 'When they take the field on Sunday I want *my* team...'

Barry frowned.

'All right, *our* team,' said Di, 'to do their best.'

Roz, Donna and Zoë led the pack of runners. Roz shook her head. 'You'd think after her scene on Saturday the woman would keep a low profile!'

'Fat chance,' said Donna. 'Thank heavens she's not our manager.'

As the tail-enders, Jason, Bugle and Matey, dragged themselves past the main gate Stan entered. He was wrapped up as though it was mid-December. He sneezed, wiped his eyes, and looked at the joggers in disbelief.

'What's going off 'ere?' he gasped.

'The 3000 metres,' said Jason. 'Thanks to the Big Noise from Barnsley.'

Stan made his way quickly to where the Higgses were standing. He blew his nose loudly. 'Cricket teams do not need cross-country. Call them in.'

Di scowled. But a flurry of sneezes from Stan seemed to impress her. 'OK,' she said softly. 'Back you come, you lot,' she roared. The pack altered course and sprinted across the field.

'You look really poorly, Stan,' said Barry with concern.

'I've just been to the doctor and he says the best place for me is bed,' said Stan.

Di almost danced with delight. 'Gather round, you lot.'

The team gathered round. Jason and Bugle flopped down on the grass.

Stan's voice was becoming even more croaky. 'This Sunday Donna will be in the team and Craig will be twelfth man.' There was a murmur of approval.

'Who'll be the scorer?' asked Scooby.

'Dot Ball says she'll do the job,' said Donna.

'Fine,' croaked Stan. 'But in all honesty I'm not going to be fit enough to take you on Sunday. I'm off to my bed.'

A blanket of silence fell. 'So who *will* be in charge on Sunday?' asked Roz.

Stan paused. 'I'm asking Mrs Higgs to take over as manager on Sunday.'

'Totalitarianism,' whispered Jason.

'Corporate raiding,' said Scooby.

''Ecky thump,' said Bal.

Di looked like a cat who had just inherited a dairy. 'Ooh, Stan, I am honoured. And I accept.' Di looked at her watch and her face turned tough. 'Right, you lot, half an hour fielding practice. And we'll have a six-a-side match tomorrow.'

'Tomorrow,' gasped Slasher.

'That's Yorkshire for you,' said Roz.

'What do you mean?' asked Lenny.

'Your mother hasn't been in charge two minutes and she's got us working overtime.' She broke into broad Yorkshire. 'If tha' don't like conditions at 'Iggs's Mill then tha' mun lump 'em.'

'I won't let you down, Stan,' stated Di slapping him soundly on the back. It set Stan off coughing violently.

'She's trying to put him out for the season,' said Malcolm.

Next morning as Lenny came down for breakfast he could hear his mother bending his father's ear about the big game.

'We need about a hundred and sixty runs. So I might put Donna up the order. Then again...'

Lenny grinned. He noticed a postcard lying on the mat in the hall. A brief glance showed that it was from Di's Auntie Mavis in Barnsley.

Di read a bit out. 'I have decided to take a trip to your home in Lancashire. Do they have electricity there yet?'

'Cheek,' snorted Barry.

'I will arrive at Slogthwaite station at 3 p.m. on Saturday. Hope this suits. Love, Auntie Mavis.' Di laughed. 'Just think, on Sunday she can come to the game and see our Leonard bat.'

And see our Di manage, thought Lenny. 'Great,' he said.

Di sat down and a funny, dreamy look came over her face. 'I'll never forget Auntie Mavis and Uncle Les taking me to Blackpool. Every year from when I was eight until I was fourteen. We always stayed at the same place, the Lyndene Guest House. They even gave me spends. I promised Auntie Mavis that one day I'd repay her. By treating her to a holiday in Blackpool.'

It pleased Lenny to see his mother in this mood. Maybe she'd be less of a pain on Sunday with Auntie Mavis around.

Di picked Geoffrey up and began to dance round the kitchen with him. 'Ooh, it's going to be a smashing weekend. Auntie Mavis is cricket daft. When Uncle Les was alive they never missed a game at Laston Rec.'

Lenny began to eat his breakfast.

'I want you at the practice tonight bang on six, Leonard,' said Di. 'You have to set an example.'

Behind her back Lenny winked at his father. 'I'm going early for extra batting practice, Mum,' he said.

'Good,' said Di. 'Barry,' she spoke in a sugar-sweet way, 'could you ring Pat Masters and ask her to drop into Sloggers this evening?'

'Why, dear?' asked Barry.

'Because I've got plans for her as well as the team.'

Lenny shuddered at the tone.

Dot Ball was a very happy lady. She was sitting beside Donna, who was wearing a track suit, and nodding approvingly as Lenny, also in a track suit, finished a piece on the violin. 'Very good,' said Dot. 'Regular practice and you'll make an excellent musician, young man.'

Lenny did not have time to bask in the praise. Quickly he put the fiddle in its case and stuck it in the bottom of Donna's cricket bag. 'Home' for the fiddle at the moment was at Donna's house.

'Congratulations on getting into the team, dear.' Dot smiled at Donna. 'I'm very pleased to be the new scorer.'

'Craig will be your tin-lad,' said Donna. 'He's very conscientious.'

'Well, let's hope the team operate as efficiently as the score-box people on Sunday.'

Lenny and Donna picked up their bags and made to leave.

'Hang on,' said Dot. 'I'm busy on Saturday morning, Lenny. So can you come round for your lesson at three o'clock?'

Lenny's face dropped. 'My mum's Auntie Mavis is due here for a holiday at three. Dad and me are going to pick her up.'

Dot frowned. 'You really do need regular lessons.'

'OK,' said Lenny. 'Me and my dad will wangle summat. But can the lesson be round at Donna's house? I've got to keep my mum off my trail.'

Dot laughed. 'All right. It strikes me if she finds out about this phantom fiddle you'll get a rocket, and I'll get sacked as scorer.'

It was like no other practice ever seen at Sloggers' ground. First of all Di made the whole team stand in a line outside the changing rooms. They lined up like this: Lenny, Scooby, Roz, Zoë, Matey, Bugle, Bal, Malcolm, Jason, Slasher, Donna and Craig.

'*Dad's Army* or what?' said Jason.

'Di's army more like,' said Scooby.

'Leonard, is everything as I ordered out there?' Di's voice echoed from the changing rooms.

'Yes, Mum,' Lenny shouted. He turned and addressed Jason and Scooby. 'Stop chelping, will you. Stan says she's the manager. Don't start crying until you're hurt.' Lenny's words hung in the air. The whole team wondered what on earth Di was preparing for them.

'In here at once, Leonard!' yelled Di.

Lenny shouted, 'Yes, Mum.'

'Yes, boss!' screamed Di.

Thirty seconds later Di and Lenny came out of the

changing rooms. Each was carrying a bundle of football training bibs.

Scooby snorted under his breath. 'Bibs! Bibs! It's not cricket. I'm going to report the woman to Lord's.'

'Shut up and give her a chance,' said Roz. Donna and Zoë nodded agreement.

Di marched along the line 'reviewing' the team. She did not seem impressed. 'Today's six-a-side practice will not be the normal slapdash job. Today we will be scientific, objective – even *brutal*.' She let the words sink in. 'I will pretend I have never seen any of you play cricket before. Lenny – I mean number one – you will captain one side. You,' she pointed at Bal, 'number seven, you will captain the other. Number one, dish out the numbers.'

Lenny obeyed.

Barry, Geoffrey and Pat Masters entered the ground. Pat looked at Di as though she was an alligator dossing on her fireside rug.

'Right,' yelled Di. 'Number one, your team, that's numbers one to six, will bat.'

As the two teams moved off, Pat gave a polite cough. 'Barry said you wanted to see me, Mrs Higgs. Do I get a number?' Pat asked sarcastically.

'No,' flashed Di. 'You get a job.' She ran into the changing rooms and came out with two long, off-white umpire's coats. She handed them to Pat and Barry. 'Stan's not well, so you two can be umpires.' The tatty coat jarred with Pat's expensive sweater and skirt. She said nowt.

The game got going with number eight, Malcolm, bowling to number two, Scooby, and number one, Lenny, the other batter. Normally the coach would watch the game from the boundary, or ten metres or so from the action. Not Di. She settled on her hands and knees at the bowler's end and watched where Malcolm's feet landed. She frowned, scribbled notes on her pad and ignored Malcolm's hostile glances.

Next over she went to gully and watched intently as Lenny shaped up to face Bal. The ball hit a divot and reared up. Lenny played it awkwardly to mid-on.

'Rubbish shot, number one,' Di screeched. 'That should have been hooked.'

Lenny jerked round through 180 degrees to look at her and there was a loud click. Something throbbed in the right side of Lenny's neck. He took guard feeling dizzy. The muscle in his neck was stiff as a post. Di breezed up and hovered over Donna who was acting as wicket-keeper. 'Bend those knees, number eleven,' yelled Di.

Donna rolled her eyes and obeyed.

'It's like painting by numbers,' said Matey as he walked past Lenny.

Lenny began to nod agreement but his neck wouldn't let him.

At the team talk an hour later Lenny really did think his mother was going over the top. Di had marked everybody in the team from one to ten. Scooby, Roz and Lenny had been given four. Everyone else had been given three, except Craig. Di had given him only two and reduced him to tears by adding that she thought he was scared of the ball.

'And he's only the tin-lad now,' said Bugle under his breath.

It crossed Lenny's mind that this was no way to raise morale before a Cup Match.

Di put away her notebook. She zipped her track suit right up to the top. She thrust out her chin and stomped to the changing-room door. 'I suggest you all go home now and digest today's lessons. I want you all to have the right *attitude* against Sandwell.'

She slammed the door.

'Right attitude. Fat chance,' said Roz.

The team sat around, shell-shocked. Lenny rubbed at the right side of his neck. The muscles were locked. He massaged the area and jumped with pain.

'Are you OK?' asked Donna.

'I'll be reet,' said Lenny. He chucked his bib on the floor beside the others. 'Hey. Maybe my mum will be a bit gentler on Sunday.'

'What makes you think that?' asked Scooby.

'Well, Auntie Mavis is coming on a visit. She's from Barnsley.'

Jason threw up his hands in despair. 'Auntie Mavis *and* your mother. Two Yorkshire ladies. I'm bringing a tin hat!'

At 2.45 on Saturday afternoon the menfolk of the Higgs household were showing signs of strain. Barry and Lenny, with some 'help' from Geoffrey, were laying on an Everest of a high tea for Auntie Mavis. The table groaned with pies, cakes, pickles, the full monty, and Geoffrey was eager to do a bit of sampling.

'Get out of it,' snapped Barry as yet another scone with cheese and chives was nicked from the pile.

'Easy, Dad,' said Lenny. 'There's enough nosh to feed Giant Haystacks and his brother.' Lenny rubbed the right side of his neck which was still giving him gyp.

'Don't rub that when your mum gets back from the hairdresser's. She'll throw a wobbler,' said Barry. He ran his hands through his hair as he always did when nervous.

'Dad?' Lenny's voice was serious. 'Do you think this plan of yours is going to work? I could ring Donna and Dot and cancel it.'

'No,' rapped Barry. 'Auntie Mavis has never been to Slogthwaite before. So while you're "missing" for an hour, I can show her the sights.'

'The park. The beck,' laughed Lenny.

'The gasworks,' added Barry.

'And, of course, the clog factory.' Lenny's mood was buoyant. The scheme would work, wouldn't it?

'I'm back, folks. Everything under control?' Di's cheery tones brought them back down to earth. With frowns of intense concentration they began pushing plates around.

'High tea detail ready for inspection,' said Lenny pompously as Di swept in.

'Time to go get Auntie Mavis,' said Barry. He and Lenny raced out to the car leaving Di preening in the mirror.

As Lenny fastened his safety belt his neck muscles ached. He could turn his head to the left OK, but not the right. It's all I need, he thought, to have to cry off on the day my mum makes her debut as manager. Barry dropped him off at Donna's house and raced on to the station to begin a one-hour mystery tour with Auntie Mavis.

Auntie Mavis was not best pleased. Thanks to a mix-up on British Rail she had arrived at Slogthwaite station half an hour early. There was no buffet about, so she had been sitting on her case stewing.

When Barry pitched up in the car at five past three he was full of good cheer. 'Hello, love,' he burbled. 'Pleasant journey?'

'I've been sat here like one o'clock half-struck, my lad. Train were *early*.' She pointed to her enormous baggy case. 'Chuck that in yer motor and let me get a drop of tea and a bit of scoff.'

Barry chose not to hear this. Even if Auntie had not eaten or drunk for a month she was going to be shown the sights of Slogthwaite.

'You've never been here before, have you?' Barry's voice was all sugar.

Auntie Mavis fastened the seat belt and looked round about her as though Slogthwaite was a jungle full of wild animals about to pounce. 'Nay. I like Blackpool, but the rest of Lancashire I wouldn't give yer tuppence for.'

That's it, thought Barry. Higgs's Tours announce the departure of flight into the unknown.

By five to four Auntie Mavis had seen more of

Slogthwaite than most lifelong residents. She finally called a halt when Barry was showing her the ducks in the park pond.

'Ducks, swans, we get the lot here...'

Auntie cut in with an icy tone. 'I'd prefer chicken.'

Barry's mouth dropped. 'Chicken. On a pond?'

'No, between two bits of bread.'

Barry drove quickly to Donna's house and banged his horn. Lenny trotted out innocently. He dutifully kissed Auntie Mavis.

'What have you been up to in there?' Auntie pointed at the house.

'Just a bit of homework, that's all.' Lenny smiled.

The bombshells began dropping after Auntie Mavis had eaten an enormous tea and given it her seal of approval. As she daintily sipped her third cup of tea, she listened to Di's plans.

'Tonight Barry will cook us another lovely meal,' gushed Di. 'Then tomorrow our Leonard's cricket team, Sloggers, are playing in the Cup. Actually I am team manager.'

Auntie Mavis had started to frown from the minute Di opened her mouth. She began to shake her head. Di stopped in her tracks. 'Anything wrong?' asked Di.

A crafty, witch-like look came over Auntie's face. 'There's no meal here for me and you tonight, lass.'

Di looked lost.

Auntie went on, 'And as for cricket, I hate the game. I only went along to watch to please your Uncle Les, rest his soul.'

Di looked as though she'd lost a hundred pounds and found a ten-pence piece.

Auntie was not finished. 'You promised me years ago that you would take me to Blackpool, our Di. So we two are off there tonight. I've got train tickets, reservations at Lyndene, and tomorrow we're going to the top of the Tower. Now isn't that far better than sitting at a silly cricket match?'

Di could hardly hold back the tears. Lenny wanted to cry himself. He jumped up from the tea table. His neck was raging with pain. He put his arm around Di's shoulders. 'Auntie, this is a very important cricket match...'

Barry broke in softly. 'But it's not as important as a promise – a solemn *promise* – made many years ago.'

Di's eyes flashed. She sniffed. 'Blackpool it is then.'

Auntie Mavis nodded happily and Lenny poured her another cuppa.

Di and Barry went into the kitchen.

'Good attitude, love,' said Barry. He kissed Di on the forehead.

'But who is going to manage the team?' asked Di.

'Me,' said Barry. 'Tha's taught me a few tricks, owld lass.'

SIX

Lenny Higgs was having a very confusing dream. Ninety per cent of it was real, but the rest was wild. His mum and Auntie Mavis had gone off to Blackpool on the 7 p.m. train. Barry had sweet-talked Pat Masters into lending him the posaphone, so Di could be kept in touch ball-by-ball with the cricket match. Barry had made a brill spaghetti bolognese and they'd all gone to bed. Then the dream went loopy. A dragon started to bite the right side of Lenny's neck, or so it seemed.

Lenny woke up with a start. He raised his head from the pillow and inched it left. No probs. But one twitch to the right and the dragon's teeth were back. Even a millimetre movement was agony. No cricket for me today, Lenny thought, I'd be a liability to the team. He flicked on his bedside lamp. It was just after 3 a.m.

Lenny got out of bed and tiptoed to his parents' room. Barry took no raising. The weight of the managership was massive. He'd drifted into a light doze. He held Lenny gently by the ears. Suddenly he grinned. 'Go get your mum's sun lamp from under the stairs. It might just do the trick.'

'It's very hot, Dad,' said Lenny ten minutes later.

Barry held the lamp closer to Lenny's neck. 'That means it's doing you good.'

After half an hour of the 'treatment' Lenny went back to bed. He went out like a light.

At 8 a.m. Barry was rustling up a bacon, egg and beans breakfast. Outside the sun shone and there was not a cloud in the sky. Barry whistled as he worked. Lenny's voice came loud and clear from the hall. 'There's kind of good news and bad, Dad.'

Barry froze. 'Give us the good first.'

Lenny walked in with his hands covering the sore part of his neck. 'The *good* news is I can now move my neck,

70

no bother. The bad news is that lamp has given me third-degree burns.'

Lenny dropped his hands. His neck was as red as a traffic light and small blisters had popped up over a five-centimetre area.

'It's all my fault,' screamed Barry. 'Your mother will kill me.'

Lenny laughed. 'Calm down, Dad. It doesn't hurt that much. It's just uncomfortable. I *can* bend my neck. And I'm going to play. We can tell Mum I fell in a bed of nettles.'

Barry was just about starting to see the funny side of the sun-lamp saga when the phone rang. They both knew who it would be. Barry put on a plastic grin and spoke as if his mouth was full of broken glass.

'Hello there, Higgs household.'

Lenny tried to stop Geoffrey hurling cereal round the kitchen as Di bent his dad's ear. Every minute or so Barry got in a word or two. 'Lovely day. Sunny.' More ear-bending. Then Barry's face dropped. 'His neck? Well, of course it's no problem. In fact our kid is just *burning* to get out there against Sandwell.'

Lenny fell about laughing. Geoffrey spooned a clot of cereal at Barry. Barry had had enough. 'Look, dear, have a lovely day with Auntie Mavis in Blackpool. I've got managership to do today. Call when the game's on.'

Barry put down the phone. 'We'll put a scarf or hanky round your burn. And with any luck the redness will have cooled by the time your mum gets home tonight.' Barry stopped speaking. He thumped the side of his head.

'What's up, Dad?' asked Lenny.

'Teas! Not only have I got to be manager, emergency burns unit operative, you name it – but what about teas?'

'We'll manage summat, manager,' said Lenny.

There was a deputation waiting in the tea-room at

Sloggers for Barry when he walked in with Geoffrey. It was a friendly one. Pat Masters, with her sidekicks Sharon and Mary, were lined up behind the counter with wide grins. At first Barry did not notice the mood. He assumed there would be panic stations over lack of arrangements for tea.

'Right, girls,' breezed Barry. 'I'm up to my eyes with jobs to do, so let's keep tea simple. Bit of salad. Bit of ham. Then, the odd scone or bit of malt loaf...'

Pat Masters bore down on Barry. She picked up Geoffrey and sat him on the counter. Barry was putting on a pinny. Pat stopped him.

'Leave the teas to us, Barry. It will not be bits and bobs. We will do our best. Geoffrey can stay with us. And here is the mobile phone you asked for.' She took the posaphone from her shopping bag. She allowed herself one dig. 'It's a shame Lady – I mean Di – is missing today. But I'm sure with the aid of this,' she handed over the phone, 'you can keep her posted – wherever she is.'

Barry bit back a retort and mumbled his thanks to the ladies. He had too much on his plate for any aggro.

In the dressing room Lenny was taking stick – and it was not from his neck. Nothing had been said about Di's change of plans, or Barry's role as manager, but when Lenny began to cover his burnt neck, the patter started. The only suitable neckwear in the Higgs household was a white silky scarf that had been given to Di as a present. Lenny wound it round his neck.

'What ho, Biggles,' cracked Bugle. 'Chocks away time, is it?'

Scooby weighed in too. 'That's the posiest thing I've ever seen, Higgsy. The Lone Ranger look, is it? What, no black mask?'

Bal caught the joky vibes. 'I have to argue, skipper. It may help your neck problem, but you look a right dollop.'

'Ten-pence fine for posy gear.' Matey scribbled in the book. Without a word Lenny paid up. He forgot to tuck the ends of the scarf into his shirt.

The door was flung open and Howarth, the Sandwell skipper, swaggered in. 'Hi-ho, Silver, away,' he said pointing to the scarf. 'You ready to toss up, Lenny?'

'In a tick,' said Lenny. He rubbed his neck. It was now stiffening up again.

Howarth went out as Barry came in. He carefully placed the posaphone on the table. Scooby looked at it.

'Does Mrs Higgs know the number?' asked Scooby.

'Yes,' said Barry sharply. Scooby looked at the ceiling. Barry got straight down to the main business of the day. 'Right, team, you all know why I'm in charge today. Stan is poorly and Di is otherwise engaged.' There were a couple of soft giggles, but Barry ignored them. 'So for the next few hours I'm IT. I want you all just to do your best. Play right in your head. Go out and WIN!'

There were no laughs. Frowns of concentration were the order of the day. Lenny sensed that his team for once were focused. The team filed out. Only Lenny and Barry were left. Lenny rubbed at his neck.

'Are you going to be OK?' asked Barry.

'It's stiff but not sore,' replied Lenny.

'Right.' Barry's voice was crisp. 'If you get the chance, field, then your neck might loosen before we bat. But however the toss goes, the decision is yours.'

'OK – boss,' said Lenny.

Barry followed him out, leaving the posaphone on the table.

At ten minutes to two the trip to Blackpool was going just dandy. After a hearty breakfast Di and Auntie Mavis had mounted a tram and gone along the Golden Mile. It was not sunny, the 'breeze' cut like a chain saw, but the look on Auntie Mavis's face made Di's disappointment at not being manager disappear. Auntie

Mavis glowed with happiness as she crunched a stick of rock. Di was happy she was keeping the promise made all those years ago. But as two o'clock, match-time, approached a little spring began to coil up in Di's stomach. She had been forced to get to a phone.

'Why are we queuing for this phone when we should be going up the Tower?' moaned Auntie.

'I just want to check the cricket score,' said Di with a pointed look at the back of the teenage lad who was hogging the pay phone. The lad bashed in another four coins. Di humphed.

It was obvious the lad was talking to his girlfriend. Di tried all the tricks to get him to hurry. She humphed, rattled coins, even coughed pointedly. It did no good. It was 2.07 before he moved away.

'Sorry, missus.' He grinned at Di. 'But you know what these Yorkshire girls are like – they'd chat for ever.'

Di did not flinch. She had the Masters' posaphone number written down. She dialled it. The number rang – and rang – and rang.

Di hung up. 'Stupid thing, must be on the blink.'

She and Auntie moved towards the Tower.

On the table in the Sloggers dressing room the posaphone rang unheeded. Barry and Co's minds were on other things. Out on the square Sandwell, and particularly their skipper Howarth, were making hay. After two overs there were twenty runs on the board for no wicket. Malcolm was trying to bowl too fast, and at the other end Slasher kept providing balls of a 'hittable length'. Barry stood by the old seat with Mr Ackroyd.

'Keep it tight,' yelled Barry.

'It's great when that loud-mouthed Yorkshire woman's missing,' commented Mr Ackroyd.

Barry said nowt.

By 2.20 things were worse. Sandwell had cruised to 40 for 0.

Lenny took the ball, rubbed his neck, and called up Roz.

'I'm going to tempt these two. I reckon they think they're going to coast this game. What do you reckon?'

Roz smiled. She took the ball. 'Temptation it is.'

Lenny moved to mid-on. He flexed his neck. It was much better. 'Catch it! Catch it, Len!' In thinking about his neck he'd forgotten about the game. Roz's dolly-drop had caused Howarth to whack the ball at Lenny. He got a hand to it. The ball thudded into his chest. Lenny bobbled the ball for a second then hung on to it.

'Howzat!' yelled Sloggers.

Up went the umpire's finger. 40 for 1.

It was hard work from then on, but every Sloggers player gave 100 per cent. When it came to the last over Sandwell were 112 for 9. A big kid was on thirty and he really knew how to whack the ball. Lenny was reviewing who should bowl the last vital six balls.

The team looked at Lenny. He walked to the bowler's end. He tightened the scarf. Roz poised in the slips.

'Come on, Lenny,' she yelled. 'Put it on the spot.'

So far I've caught a decapitation job, bent, run, twisted and kept the team's heads up, thought Lenny. So now let's see if I can keep the runs down.

Lenny's first three balls drew wild yahoo swipes from the batter. None connected. The fourth ball screamed back at Lenny and he thrust out a hand. The ball stuck. Regardless of his poorly neck, the Sloggers' lot mobbed him. They now needed 113 to win.

When the merry throng entered the dressing room with Barry their cheers died in their throats. The posaphone was ringing loudly.

Barry picked it up and began to talk to Di.

Auntie Mavis had played a blinder. Laden with rock, balloons and wearing silly hats, Di and she had made their way to the top of the Tower. As Di admired the view there were shrieks from behind her: Auntie Mavis was throwing a wobbler.

'Ooh, ooh, I feel all giddy, our Di. Take me 'ome. I'd rather be at that daft cricket game than up here.' Mavis was as pale as a sheet.

Now Di was at the railway station in a phone box.

'How are we doing?' she asked.

'Splendid,' replied Barry confidently. 'Sandwell got a hundred and twelve and we are going to knock 'em off easily. Aren't we, team?'

There was a roar of assent.

'Well, here's my advice,' said Di pompously. 'Open with a SCREEEE ...' The posaphone began to whistle. Barry put it down with a grin.

'The order will be Lenny and Roz to open.'

Scooby banged his bat on the floor.

Barry smiled and patted his shoulder. 'Scooby, I see you as a blue-chip investment at number three. I want you to weigh up the – er – market. Be cavalier or cautious as conditions demand.'

Scooby was impressed. 'Sound, sound as a pound, Bazza.'

'I'll play it by ear from there,' said Barry. 'Now let's relax and have tea.'

The kids all trooped out. Barry and Lenny were last out. The posaphone began to ring. Lenny chucked a spare sweater over it. He and his father went to tea.

Twenty minutes later Roz and Lenny walked out to open the Sloggers' innings. Throughout tea Roz had been aware that there was more wrong with Lenny than a stiff, burnt neck. He was as twitchy as a hedgehog with fleas.

As polite applause and the odd cheer ushered them to the square, Lenny stopped suddenly. Roz put her hand on his shoulder. 'What's up?'

Lenny would not look her straight in the face. 'I don't feel all that confident today. Do you mind facing?'

Roz laughed. 'No probs. Just pace yourself. I'll go for the bad balls.'

Roz walked confidently to the striker's end. She asked for a middle-stump guard. Howarth motioned two close fielders to move in a smidgen. 'On yer toes, lads. Crowd this *female*.'

The fourth ball of the over nearly produced a disaster. Roz flicked a ball off her pads and it went to an open space. 'Run,' she yelled.

'No,' yelled Lenny. He hesitated, then saw Roz galloping down the wicket. He sprinted and dived in. The keeper had the stumps down in a flash.

'Howzat?' yelled Sandwell. The umpire shook his head.

Barry, who was standing near the score-box with Zoë and Scooby, threw his head in his hands.

'Easy run there,' said Scooby. 'Lenny's in a tiz.'

Zoë nodded. 'He looks more nervous than I've ever seen him.'

Barry lost a bit of his control. 'What are you playing at, our Len?' he yelled.

Pat Masters had crept up behind him. 'If you ask me,' Pat said venomously, 'we are witnessing a rebellion. When your wife stands and shouts Lenny obeys. This is his way of showing his true feelings.'

'Rubbish,' said Barry. 'The lad's got a poorly neck, a big job and ...' He broke off. Lenny was staring like a lost sheep at the old seat. Barry twigged. He mumbled softly to himself, 'Our kid does not need shouting and bawling from the old seat – he just needs a presence there, a focus.'

Barry ran off leaving Pat with mouth agape. He slowed to a casual walk as he approached the seat. He waved and caught Lenny's eye. 'Calm down,' Barry mouthed. Lenny's face lit up. He stroked the next ball for two.

'That's it, young Higgsy,' shouted Mr Ackroyd. 'Stop playing get-out shots. Show us your strokes.'

Lenny crashed a cover drive past Howarth. He hooked the next ball for four.

'That's the stuff, Lenny,' shouted Matey. He put the fines book back in his cricket bag.

Half an hour into the Sloggers' innings things were going great. Roz was holding one end up and Lenny was going for his shots at the other. Roz had fifteen on the board and Lenny thirty-nine. Lenny steered a ball to mid-on, they took a quick run and Lenny had pinched the bowling.

The rest of the Sloggers' team lounged in the pleasant sunlight and clapped languidly. Jason put down the Sunday paper and grinned. 'My horoscope says I should venture forth and be brave...'

'... and get out first ball,' said Bal. 'You can take your pads off, Jacey baby. You won't be batting today.'

There were murmurs of assent as Lenny played a perfect straight drive for four. The scoreboard rattled up fifty-nine as Di and Auntie Mavis, laden with balloons and bags and still in daft hats, raced on to the ground. Di dragged Auntie round the boundary to where Barry was standing by the old seat.

Di's voice was quivery. 'Is it our Lenny who's on forty-four?' she asked, pointing at the scoreboard.

'Aye.' said Barry. 'Should get his fifty, no bother.'

Lenny had his back to them as he checked the score. He turned to face the new bowler. One end of the white scarf had become untucked and now it fluttered in the wind.

Di's smile vanished. 'What on earth is that round our Lenny's neck?'

Barry sucked in air. Lenny was looking at him for guidance. It was no time for up-and-downies with Di. He motioned a steady shot to Lenny.

'Can I just say that we had a problemette and we sorted it out, dear?' The pleading in his voice got through to Di. She kissed him on the cheek. 'I might have known my menfolk could handle the pressure of today. Come on, Auntie.'

Barry was amazed as they went off towards the club-house. In the middle Lenny played two balls defensively. Outside the clubhouse Matey and Bal were cheering Lenny on.

'That's the style, lads,' said Di, giving them each a stick of rock and her and Mavis's daft hats. 'Come on, Sloggers,' she shouted in a pale apology for her usual holler. Bal and Matey stood open-mouthed. As Di and Auntie Mavis entered the clubhouse Lenny rattled a four past square leg. He was now on forty-eight.

The excitement on the pitch had percolated to the tea-ladies. Pat and her cronies were in their pinnies, yelling through the picture window. Di walked quietly to the counter, put on a pinny and began to wash up.

Even Auntie Mavis was swept up in the atmosphere. She pressed her nose to the window. 'Come over and watch, our Di. Leonard wants two for his fifty. Clog it, our kid!'

Pat and Co turned with shamed faces. Geoffrey left Pat's side and ran to his mum. She gave him some rock and kept her head down over the dishes.

'We know you're no shirker, Di Higgs, come and watch,' said Pat tightly.

Di did not look up from the sink. 'Who cares if my lad's out now? The *team* will win the match. In fact I reckon Scooby is due some big runs today.'

A hearty 'Howzat' echoed from outside. 'Lenny's out,' said Pat. 'Caught on the boundary. Almost a six.'

'He did the right thing. Obviously he was going for them and Roz is our sheet anchor.' Di began to dry pots. 'Obviously this team hardly needs a manager.' She did not even blush.

Di's prophesy was right on the button. On the pitch it was no contest. Scooby batted like a man inspired. In the next twenty minutes Roz scored only two runs, and Scooby raced to forty-four. With the home crowd going bananas, Scooby lofted the next ball over the bottom wall for six. Sloggers had won with only one wicket down.

Di Higgs, holding an excited Geoffrey, and Auntie Mavis, now a convert to cricket, stayed behind the tea-counter as Scooby received the Man of the Match award. 'Speech, speech,' yelled the Sloggers kids but Scooby seemed miles away. He mumbled a brief thanks then went to his cricket coffin and opened the lid. Furtively he touched a big book lying on his spare bat. Its title was *Legends of the Norsemen*. Something like a smile flickered over his face. He tossed the trophy in and closed the lid.

'What's he playing Joe Cool for?' asked Matey pointing at Scooby.

'He's probably got his mind on some new scheme to make him a millionaire,' said Jason.

Pat Masters was now clucking round Scooby like a broody hen.

On the other side of the room, behind the counter, the Higgs family was having a showdown. A bit of the old bile crept back into Di's tones as she faced down Barry and Lenny. 'Tek off that silly scarf and let's have the full story,' rasped Di.

Lenny did. The right side of his neck glowed red like a traffic light.

Di gasped. 'That's never sunburn...'

Barry cut in. 'Well, it is, dear, in a way. Lenny's neck stiffened up, so I got out your old lamp. Turned it up too high and...'

'... best neck of Higgs, very well done,' said Lenny. 'Me dad was just doing his best. It looked like I would miss the game.'

For a moment Di's face was set. Then up piped Auntie Mavis. 'The last time I seen flesh like that was when my Les spilled a boiling kettle over his corns.'

The Higgses, as one, began to laugh. Lenny walked over to his coffin and opened the lid. He began tucking the scarf under his pads. Suddenly he cried out, ''Ere, you lot, he's struck again.'

The team crowded round as Lenny held up a cardboard box hidden under his gear. 'The Pie Piper,' he gasped.

Lenny opened the lid of the box to reveal twelve pork pies and a note. Roz picked it up and read: 'This is by ways of thanks for the rock, the pop and, of course, the usual excellent tea. Signed, the Pie Piper.'

Roz looked round at the throng. Some of the kids were still sucking the rock Di and Auntie Mavis had supplied in abundance. 'He's been here today. He could be in this room now.' She rolled her eyes. Only Scooby had stayed where he was. The group round Lenny's coffin eyed him suspiciously. Scooby sneered.

Lenny began to munch a pie. 'This is war. I will not rest until I reveal the Pie Piper.' Nobody added to this. They were all busy scrabbling for the Piper's latest offering.

SEVEN

For once Lenny Higgs's complex life was letting him off the hook. He was chuffed to pieces at his mother's behaviour at the Sandwell match. Maybe now she realised that he did not need verbal fireworks to play cricket to the best of his ability. As long as Di or Barry was at the fixed point on the boundary, Lenny could settle and do his thing. It was like a little kid having a blanket.

Stan had come round to the Higgses' house two days after the match and congratulated them all. 'Great family effort in the Cup,' was his comment. Then he took Lenny to one side and asked him to form a working party to dig a drain at the ground.

Now, on Wednesday night at just after eight, Lenny was on his way to Scooby's shed. Why the shed? Lenny wondered. Scooby had sounded very furtive on the phone. 'Just get down here. I've got to talk to you,' Scooby had said.

Lenny was planning to fit in a violin practice at Donna's house after his talk with Scooby. And his mind was brimming with great ideas, straight out of *'Allo, 'Allo* to catch the Pie Piper. He whistled a bit of Vivaldi as he jogged happily towards Scooby's house.

Scooby's shed glowed like a set for *Hallowe'en III*. An eerie light came through the window and the crack where the door was ajar. A voice inside seemed to be involved in a ritualistic chant. The voice was Scooby's.

'And in the winter of his years Slog the Norseman did truly amaze the villagers of Slogthwaite, the settlement he had founded.' Scooby's voice was that of a lad possessed.

His face creased in a grin, Lenny looked in the window. Scooby was in overalls and had wood-shavings in his hair. He was sitting on a stool reading an old book. The light of an Anglepoise lamp showed bits of wood and a lathe.

'Slog cut the end off an oar from his long-sunk long-ship and used it to strike a ball to all parts of Green Bottom,' Scooby chanted on.

Lenny covered his mouth to stop laughing out loud.

'So, who can tell, Slog the Norseman could have founded cricket in Lancashire in the year 890...'

'The same year as the Oswaldtwhistle Flying Pig Extravaganza. Load of rubbish,' said Lenny loudly.

Scooby shut the book and pointed the lamp at Lenny. Lenny moved inside the shed. 'What are you sitting in this mess for when there's things to do? The Pie Piper...'

Scooby brushed shavings from his hair and overalls. He glowered at Lenny. 'Rubbish! Mess!' Scooby thundered. 'This project could make our fortunes. So don't you scoff, Higgsy.'

The word 'our' set off dark bells in Lenny's head, but all he said was, 'You're off your trolley!'

Scooby switched off the lamp. In the pitch blackness of the shed Lenny heard him shuffling around moving bits of gear. Suddenly Scooby began to hum the *Mastermind* TV theme. There was a click, the lamp came on – to reveal Scooby's secret passion. A spanking new cricket bat was held in a vice like Excalibur in the rock. Down the side of the splice were the words 'The Scooby Norseman'. Below was pasted a sticker of a fierce Norseman in a horned helmet.

Scooby's voice quivered. 'The Scooby Norseman. Blade of champions. Conceived in the murky twilight of pre-history. Born...'

'In a shed in Slogthwaite.' Lenny's voice was as flat as a paving-stone.

Scooby, wild-eyed, took the bat from the vice and held it aloft. 'You've no imagination, our Leonard. I feel like Columbus sighting the New World or McDonald when he invented the hamburger!'

Lenny shook his head sadly. This boy is away with the mixer, he thought.

Scooby's voice changed tone to flat calm, the sort that comes before a storm. 'Making bats is slow, precision work, Len. So I need a partner.'

The word did not sound friendly to Lenny.

Scooby continued, 'I will be in charge of design, production and marketing.' He took off the overalls to reveal a gleaming white shirt, tie and natty braces. 'And of course I will be MD.'

'Boss,' said Lenny, still half-convinced that this was a joke.

'Boss? Yes,' drawled Scooby. 'You will be my engine room.'

'Slave?' asked Lenny, now reckoning the joke was wearing thin.

'Er – working partner,' said Scooby. 'Agreed?' He stuck out his hand. Lenny refused to shake it.

'Look, Scoob,' said Lenny reasonably. 'I'll help you with the bat-making. But it's just a hobby. We've got cricket to play and loads of other things to do.' He stuck out his hand. 'I'll shake hands, if you get your priorities right. Cricket first, OK?'

Scooby would not shake. He clutched the bat to his chest. 'I warn you that this could mean bother, Len,' said Scooby.

Lenny had had enough. He walked out of the shed and headed for Donna's.

An hour later Lenny finished a practice on the violin and Donna was impressed. She put the school fiddle away and gave Lenny her opinion. 'I think you're going to get into that orchestra, no sweat.' She handed Len a letter from Dot Ball. Lenny's face went from happy to miserable in about ten seconds flat.

'The good news is that I've got to go to the auditions,' said Lenny.

'Great!' said Donna. 'And...'

'The bad news is that the auditions are in Preston at three p.m. on Saturday.'

'Right in the middle of our game with Rycliffe!'

Donna frowned. 'You've got to go. We can win without you.'

Outside the open window a beady pair of eyes rolled then narrowed. Scooby was hiding in a rhododendron bush. He had come to check that the fiddle was still at Donna's, but news of the auditions made him smile – evilly.

'Enough of my problems, girl,' said Lenny. 'I've just been to see Scooby and he's gone potty about his bat-making. He wants me to be his partner.'

Donna groaned. 'You don't think he'll pack up cricket 'cos of his new passion, do you?'

'No, even Scoob wouldn't go that far,' Lenny said.

'We'll see about that, *partner*,' hissed Scooby as he shifted quietly off into the night.

By 6.15 on Wednesday evening Lenny was not even remotely near hatching an excuse to miss Saturday's match. So he was not exactly giving Stan 100 per cent attention as Stan addressed the working party about the digging of the drain trench by the old seat.

'Right. Take this piece of string,' said Stan. Bugle, Malcolm and Bal leapt into action, but Lenny was miles away. 'Come on, Lenny, frame yourself,' rasped Stan.

Lenny joined the others in laying string along the line they would have to dig up. Across on the pitch itself Di was taking the rest of the team for fielding practice. There was no sign of Matey or Scooby. The latter's absence worried Lenny considerably.

'I could've done with Scooby being here on time,' muttered Stan. 'He's a dab hand at woodwork and I was counting on him to help shore up this trench.'

A small figure in big overalls came running over the pitch. It was Matey and he was carrying a letter in his hand. Stan and the working party stopped and gathered round him.

'Scooby came to my house and told me to give you this, Stan.' Matey handed over the envelope. As

Stan read the letter, Lenny looked worried. Di led the fielding lot over. Donna looked gravely at Lenny. Stan stopped reading and looked nonplussed. 'Just listen to this lot,' he said. He began to read. 'From Norseman Products, Registered Office 15a Morecambe Way, Slogthwaite...'

'15a?' said Zoë.

'Scooby's shed!' explained Donna.

Stan went on. 'Dear "customer", that's been crossed out. Dear Mr Topping. I regret to say that my connection with Slogthwaite CC is now terminated. I have recently embarked on a business career and have no time for fripperies...'

'What's fripperies?' asked Matey.

'Games, pastimes – like cricket,' said Malcolm.

'You watch it, young man,' yelped Di.

'... like cricket,' echoed Stan.

'He's nowt but a cheeky dollop,' shouted Di. 'Wait till I see him, and his mother.'

'That's the point, Mother,' sighed Lenny. 'We are not going to be seeing either of them.'

'So in concluding,' Stan read, 'I thank you for your comradeship and hope we can do business in the future.' Stan balled up the letter and threw it away. 'Young idiot.'

As the group began to discuss Scooby's madness, Lenny's mind swam with problems. With Scooby absent, how could he ever make a case for missing the Rycliffe game himself? Roz and Matey brought him back to the present by dragging him off to the old seat. They said they had a plan...

The plan was based on a deputation of three – Lenny, Roz and Matey – going round to Scooby's shed after the practice, and appealing to his better nature. But once the trio stepped inside 'Norseman Products', they realised that they were facing an enormous task. The big-biz bug had really bitten Scooby. The kids looked round in wonder at sales graphs and charts, a map of the world with coloured pins in target areas. Copies of *The Financial Times* littered the premises. There were even two large coloured posters of Richie Richardson and David Gower wielding the Scooby Norseman.

'He's been busy, that's for sure,' said Matey.

'How many bats has he made?' asked Roz.

'One,' said Lenny. 'It's a slow job,' he added by way of explanation.

There was a movement behind them and a vision straight out of Wall Street walked in carrying the proto-type bat. Scooby had a suit on, waistcoat and hair slicked back.

'Slow is correct,' he said acidly. 'But making bats is going to be a profitable job.' He looked at Lenny. 'Isn't it, *partner?*'

Roz and Matey shuddered. 'What's he on about, Lenny?' asked Roz.

'You don't think I'd join the loony?' Lenny protested. He turned to Scooby and his voice was all sweet reason. 'Come on, Scooby. Play cricket and we'll all give you a hand with the hobby ...'

'Hobby! Hobby!' Scooby was almost frothing at the mouth. 'This enterprise will make my fortune – and yours, Leonard Higgs.'

Roz stuck her face in Scooby's. 'I hope your stupid bat gets dry rot.' With that she stormed out.

Matey's contempt was of equal power, but the delivery was not so polished. 'I hope you get taken over by a Japanese conglo – conglom – big firm,' he spluttered.

Lenny prepared a sad, dignified exit. He shook his head and turned towards the door.

'Not so fast, Leonard, me owld pal.' Scooby was tapping his fingers on the bat. He pointed at the as yet unattached blade and handle of the new bat. 'Why don't you start work on the Scooby Norseman Number Two?'

'You must be daft,' said Lenny.

'If you don't join me, owld pal,' Scooby's face was a mask, 'your mother is going to find out about secret fiddle practices round at Donna's – and a special trip to Preston on Saturday.'

Lenny's world collapsed. 'You wouldn't,' he gasped.

'Oh yes I would – *partner*,' said Scooby. His face eased a trifle. 'But if you work Friday night and Saturday morning, I might let you off for a couple of hours on Saturday afternoon. You could keep your, er – *appointment* in Preston.'

Lenny's brains whirled. There was now some light in his life. He could wangle Preston and keep Scooby happy, but what about the reaction of his mother and the rest of Sloggers' lot to him missing a game?

Friday night cricket practice ended at ten to seven. Stan seemed pleased as he surveyed his charges all flopped on the grass. 'We don't need Scooby. Remember, we are a team,' said Stan.

Wait till he finds out I'm missing tomorrow, thought Lenny.

'Lenny,' Stan shouted. He's a mind reader, Lenny thought. 'Here's the keys. Lock up all the gear once you've got changed. See you all tomorrow at one sharp.' Stan walked off to examine the drain trench. There was an excited buzz among the team.

'So it's all systems go tonight?' asked Matey.

Lenny held up the keys and nodded.

Stan paused by the trench. It now reached four metres behind the old seat and was about a metre deep. 'Could do with being a bit deeper,' Stan said to himself before moving off.

Once Stan was out of the main gate, the gang crowded round Lenny. Despite his mountain of problems he was smiling about Operation Pie Piper.

'What's the master plan, Sherlock?' asked Slasher.

Lenny jingled the keys. 'The Pie Piper is a master of subterfuge, probably disguise and, above all, split-second timing. He always strikes *before* a match. He must know we are on his trail – so I reckon he will put his pies in place *tonight*.'

Lenny had his audience ensnared. 'So, at half-past nine tonight we will return to the ground, hide out in various places, pounce and expose him.'

'Where do we hide exactly?' asked Matey.

Lenny paused. The team stirred uneasily. 'Well – I reckon you can work that out yourselves. You see, I can't make it tonight. My mum would go nuts if I moved out of the house after nine. So it's up to you lot.' He chucked the keys to Jason. 'Lock up at twelve o'clock, whatever happens.'

Leaving most of the team speechless, Lenny shot off.

'He's not going fiddle-practising, is he?' Roz glared at Donna.

'He's not going to join Scooby making silly bats, is he?' asked Matey.

'Does it matter?' asked Jason airily. 'We can catch the fiendish Pie Piper without Higgsy.'

They mooched off towards the changing rooms. Donna was convinced Lenny was off to think up a way of getting to Preston. But wasn't he leaving it a bit late?

By 9.30 Scooby was very impressed by Lenny's attitude. He had been working on the new bat for two hours solid and had doggedly refused to break for a cuppa.

'Come on, Len, pack in for a tick and have a brew,' pleaded Scooby.

The only break I'm thinking of is your neck, pal, Lenny thought as he shaved viciously at the blade of the bat.

Scooby jumped across the shed at him. 'Don't gouge the wood, Len. You could sabotage the whole effect.'

A sudden inspiration made Lenny grin. He stopped work and accepted a cup of tea.

'You'll need to show off the bat to customers soon,' said Lenny craftily.

'No sweat,' Scooby beamed. 'I'm taking my stall to Sloggers tomorrow and taking orders.'

'Very good,' said Lenny. 'Really, a full public demonstration of the Scooby Norseman would be brill.'

Scooby rose to the bait. 'We'll work on that after tomorrow, partner. By the way, do you want me to "explain your absence" when I get there?'

'Yes,' said Lenny gratefully. 'Just say I'm otherwise engaged.'

At the same time that night the Sloggers lot gathered to stake out the ground. As the rest moved to their agreed positions, Jason and Craig pulled a large tarpaulin out from behind the pavilion. Like the rest, both lads were in black gear, and Jason had black smears of soot on his face. They fumbled with the tarpaulin in the pitch blackness. Jason checked that he had his whistle on a piece of string.

'Look,' he said bossily to Craig, 'when we find him, I whistle to alert the others, and you chuck that over him.'

'You'll have to help me with the chucking, chuck,' said Craig. 'This cricket covering is heavy. And any road, why can't we just stick a needle in the Pie Piper, and send him to sleep? Or clock him with a bat?'

Jason snorted. ''Cos we want him conscious and able to confess, stupid.'

Each tugging a corner of the tarpaulin they crawled off towards the score-box. Inside, Malcolm was not exactly taking the operation seriously. He was making Freddie Kruger shadows on the back wall using light from a street-lamp. Slasher was pretending to mock but was in fact scared stiff. Jason tore Malcolm off a strip, and he and Craig crawled on.

Bugle, face blackened with cork, was peering out of the changing-room window. He held a large torch.

'Anything to report?' whispered Jason.

'No' said Bugle. ''Ere,' he turned to Matey who was meant to be on action-alert at the other window, 'owt doing?'

Nothing came from Matey but the soft buzz of snoring. Bugle switched on the torch.

'Great,' said Jason. 'On duty less than half an hour, and he turns the stake-out into a flake-out.'

'Wait till he goes on about fines to me,' snarled Bugle.

Next call for the tarpaulin squad was the clubhouse porch, which was being manned by Roz and Zoë.

'Anything occurring here?' asked Jason. Roz was opening her mouth to answer when there was a soft metallic click and the kids froze. Someone had come in the main gate and was now coming towards the porch. The light of a torch sprayed out over the pitch. Roz and Co dropped flat on the floor of the porch. The tarpaulin crackled in the wind. The beam of light played on the tarpaulin and then arced towards the porch.

Roz whispered to Jason. 'We'll grab him. You rush out and fling the tarpaulin over him.'

Jason and Craig dived past the bulky figure holding the torch. Roz and Zoë sprang.

'What's going off here?' The shocked tones were those of Di Higgs. She switched on the porch light. Roz and Zoë were frozen like two crazed statues. Jason and Craig clutched the ends of the tarpaulin.

Roz's wits were the quickest. 'We were about to cover the wicket for tomorrow's game.'

Di took off her bobble hat, and wiped sweat from her brow. She groaned. 'Covering the wicket at half-past ten at night...'

'It were on the news,' chipped in Zoë. 'Heavy showers possible.'

Di looked at the black clothes they were all wearing. Jason's sooty face caught her eye. 'So why the fancy dress?'

'Hallowe'en Disco,' blurted out Jason. 'We thought we'd have a dress run.'

'Yeah,' said Zoë. 'Formation boogie. We've been practising.'

She started to dance. Jason improvised his own steps.

Di looked at them as though they were crazy. A couple of light drops of rain fell on them. Quick as a flash the four kids dragged the tarpaulin on to the square.

'Good attitude. And good thinking,' Di shouted. 'If you see our Leonard tell him to get home sharpish. And don't forget to lock up!'

As Di's torch flickered off towards Green Lane, Jason sighed with relief. 'Good job we didn't pounce on her.'

'True,' said Craig. He yawned. 'Do you think we should go home?'

'No,' said Roz. 'We'll give it another hour.'

At half-past ten even the energies of Scooby Masters were running low. Lenny noticed this and bent over the Scooby Norseman Number Two like a beaver, but a beaver with a crafty grin.

'Knock off now if you like, Len?' There was a greasy mock mateyness in the voice that Lenny knew all too well. 'I'll pop down to Sloggers tomorrow and put the bats on display. I'll say you're off working for me.' Len forced a sour grin and nod of agreement. Scooby patted Lenny's shoulder. 'There'll be a bit of a row. But they'll buy our merchandise, and we'll condescend to show them how to use it – soon.'

Scooby stretched and yawned. Lenny's mind was working overtime. ''Bye. I just want to finish the handle,' said Lenny.

''Bye,' said Scooby. 'Keen as mustard now, aren't you?'

Scooby left.

Lenny set down the bits of bat. Mentally he ticked off his list of priorities for the next eighteen or so hours. One: hoodwink Mum. Two: brief Dad on the current ops. Three: get to and from the orchestra audition as quickly as possible. He smiled at the thought of Four: give Scooby just enough rope...

At a quarter to eleven Operation Pie Piper was about to

fizzle out due to exhaustion. The stake-out positions had been abandoned and the group of commandos were flopped on the tarpaulin just inside the main gate. Suddenly the gate squeaked on its hinges and a shadowy figure clumped to the old seat. It bent towards the drain trench. The kids froze as a dull thumping started in the trench.

'It's the Pie Piper burying his treasure just like an old buccaneer,' said Bal.

Roz, as usual, took command. 'When I get to three, blow that whistle,' she said to Jason.

'One – two – three – '

The tarpaulin squad grabbed the corners and raced to the trench. The shadowy figure had both feet inside it. The kids wrapped the intruder in the tarpaulin. Jason, Matey, Bal and Craig sat on the corners and muffled cries came from underneath.

Roz lifted up a section in the middle. 'Come out and reveal yourself, you sneaky wassock!'

Stan's head appeared from under the tarpaulin. He blinked as Zoë switched on a torch. 'I come down here to get a bit of digging done without mythering kids or gobby parents and all I get is wrapped up like a bag of chips!'

Roz flapped her lips.

'Button it, young woman. Or you'll be batting at number eleven till you get your bus pass!'

EIGHT

The fun started at Sloggers' ground about one hour before the game with Rycliffe. Knowing that the visitors had a coach who was a stickler for punctuality, Scooby had set his stall out early. Dressed in his Wall Street outfit he had erected a striped awning and under it had carefully placed Scooby Norseman bats One and Two. He had put up posters of famous cricketers, including Richie Richardson and W. G. Grace, using the bat. Already a couple of the Rycliffe lot had shown interest. Now, even though the coach had called them off for practice drill, Scooby was spieling the patter at the top of his voice to Mr Ackroyd, Mr Ackroyd's dog and the man who delivered the barm cakes.

'Roll up, roll up,' yelled Scooby. 'I am now taking orders for one of the finest bits of cricketing willow ever conceived.' Scooby holding Norseman One aloft. 'You'll never regret the purchase of a Scooby Norseman. Designed by myself, and honed to perfection by my partner, Leonard Henry Higgs.'

These last words hit Donna, Roz and Zoë like a shower of sleet as they entered the ground. A blanket of suspicion dropped over Roz and Zoë's faces. Donna bit her lip. Something told her Lenny would be off to the orchestra auditions, but what would be his excuse? Scooby left the three of them in no doubt.

'Hi, fans,' smiled Scooby. 'You'd better tell Stan he's got problems today. Not only am I unavailable, but Lenny Higgs is off on Norseman Products' business.'

Donna's teeth nearly drew blood on her lip. She hoped that Lenny was using his time on the train to and from Preston to plan Scooby's downfall. There was also the fact that even with ten players they could probably beat Rycliffe.

Roz thought it was a joke. 'Don't be daft, Scooby

Masters. Lenny Higgs wouldn't miss a match. His mother would kill him.'

The girls began to march off.

'Mark my words, ladies,' shouted Scooby. 'Our Leonard will not show his face here today.'

At ten to two the significance of Scooby's words was beginning to sink in. Stan prowled the dressing room like an ancient tiger. The kids sat round in a very subdued mood. Matey made a pathetic attempt to lift a smidgen of the gloom. He pulled the fines book from his pocket.

'Right, mateys. I'm going to fine Scooby fifty pence for bad attitude, and Lenny Higgs a pound for dereliction of duty. What do you say?'

A thunderous silence greeted the words. Roz and Bugle were both padded up to bat. Stan sighed and put on the white umpire's coat. 'It's a sad day and no mistake,' he said. 'Skipper's done a runner, star batter is going on like a demented ice-cream salesman, and Sloggers put out a ten-man team. It's a sad day in the club's history.' He patted Roz on the shoulder. 'Do your best, skip.' Stan walked out.

'Come on, lads. On yer toes.' Rycliffe clattered out of the dressing room next door. Roz got to her feet.

'Right,' she growled. 'Let's show Scooby-Rotten-Masters *and* Lenny-Rotten-Higgs.'

'Don't jump to conclusions.' Donna went red-faced. 'Lenny might have his reasons.'

Roz opened the door. Scooby's voice echoed over the ground. 'Norseman Bats will make your day.'

There was worse. Di Higgs came pelting round the boundary. 'Roz! Roz! Where's Lenny?'

Roz pointed to Donna. 'Ask her, Mrs Higgs. I've got other things on my mind.'

Roz and Bugle walked slowly to the middle. Donna allowed herself to be led aside by a fevered Di. As Di let loose the torrent Donna could not look her straight in the eye.

'Our Lenny left the house at half-past twelve. I'd ironed his whites. He had his coffin all packed ...' If she only knew about the fiddle, thought Donna. Di ranted on. 'Where is he? Is this a joke?' Suddenly Donna felt desperately sorry for the woman.

Donna pointed across the ground to Scooby and his stall. 'All I can say is I think Lenny has worked out a way of getting Scooby back into the team.' In the middle Bugle was taking a second swipe at a ball – and missing. Rycliffe were laughing at him. 'You can't say we don't *need* Scooby,' Donna added.

Di, for once in her life, was speechless. The worry about Lenny's absence seemed to disappear. In the middle a new bowler sent a bouncer round Roz's ears. Roz flailed at it. A top-edge took the ball over the slips to the boundary.

'Keep shots like that till later,' screeched Di. She made off towards the old seat.

Donna heaved a sigh of relief. At least that's got her off my case, she reflected. And I hope you've worked out the answers to a lot of awkward questions, Leonard Higgs, wherever you are.

The 1.40 train from Slogthwaite to Preston via Blackburn was not having one of its most efficient journeys. It had turned up at Slogthwaite Station twenty minutes late, and was now stuck a couple of miles outside Ramsbottom due to 'engineering difficulties'. Lenny sat with his coffin on the floor and looked out over the valley. It was a warm, sunny afternoon and despite the heat haze he could see a cricket match in progress on a small field by a stream. He was consumed with guilt. What about the team? What about Stan? What about his mates?

'Do you want a mint, love?' An old lady sitting opposite him took the packet from her handbag.

'No thanks,' said Lenny. He tried deep breathing to calm himself down. The auditions were not till 4 p.m. So with any luck he would not be too late. But ... then I've got to go back home and face another kind of music, he brooded. There was only one way to take his mind off his problems. He opened the coffin and dug through the pile of bats, pads and white clothes. He pulled out the fiddle and began to work on the test piece, 'Hungarian Dance'. Gradually the music and the rhythmic movement of the train as it set off again calmed Lenny down. He was in a world of his own as the fifty-pence piece landed with a clink in the coffin.

The old lady beamed. 'Eeh, that's lovely, young man. Do you do requests?'

A disaster of unheard-of proportions was unfolding at Sloggers. Roz could not take her mind off Scooby's relentless sales patter at his stall by the gate. She belted a ball in the second over straight back to the bowler and was caught. That made Sloggers 7 for 1.

The innings then became a miserable and embarrassing parade. Hardly had Slasher settled in at the opposite end than Bugle tried to knock the case off the ball and was bowled all over the place. 7 for 2 and Rycliffe were doing high-fives.

Malcolm hoisted a four and a six but it was merely a gesture. The side were all out for thirty-five, with only a grafting eight by Donna the slightest bright spark in ten overs.

Tea was taken in absolute silence. Rycliffe said they would not bother taking tea, since they preferred to have theirs at home once they had knocked the runs off. Di sat on the old seat and seethed silently. Barry kept his mouth buttoned as Geoffrey helped him serve the teas. Pat Masters stayed overdressed and aloof at a distant part of the boundary. Stan looked ready to commit suicide.

Only Scooby Masters had anything to say. 'Good job this is only a friendly,' he said to Roz as Sloggers prepared to field. 'If you could persuade Stan to buy a couple of my bats for the club's use, things might pick up.'

'Get lost,' was Roz's reply.

By 4 p.m. Lenny Higgs was a bundle of nerves. He ran down the corridors of the church hall the auditions were being held in, veering all over with the weight of his coffin. At last he saw a door marked 'Youth Orchestra Auditions'. He went in and saw a music stand with the test piece on it and a chair. He did not notice a sheet of paper on the chair. He took out the violin case and set it on the floor.

By instinct he picked up his favourite cricket bat. Imagining he was back at Sloggers facing the Rycliffe bowling, he tried a hook. 'It's a bouncer, but Higgs times the shot to perfection. Four jocks!'

A man and a woman each with clipboards came in and were more than slightly surprised to see this kid, his black box, and his bat round his ears. Lenny flushed, put down the bat, and took his fiddle out of the case. He still did not notice the sheet of paper on the chair.

To cover his embarrassment Lenny burbled as he tuned up. 'Me dad says music and cricket *can* mix. But me mam says no way! Nice day we've got for it, any road. Shall I start now?'

The man smiled; the woman frowned; both nodded. Leonard Henry Higgs shut his eyes and began to play.

Rycliffe passed the Sloggers' total of thirty-five without losing a wicket. It was sheer humiliation. Roz shook hands with the captain. She did not have the heart to face Stan, Di Higgs or the rest of the team. She walked over the ground to where Scooby was still relentlessly plugging the Scooby Norseman. Four of the Rycliffe team, already changed out of whites, were paying attention.

'Thirty-five quid is a snip for these bats.' Scooby held one out and a Rycliffe lad brandished it. 'Perfect weight.' Scooby saw Roz. 'Get a couple of these, darlin', and your team won't collapse.'

The Rycliffe lads grinned.

Roz wanted to cry. She fancied Lenny Higgs rotten. She knew he must have his reasons for dipping out. But why pile all the pressure on her? She brushed away a tear.

When he finished the test piece only one thing was on Lenny's mind: catching the 5 p.m. train back to Slog-thwaite. As the two officials scribbled on their pads he packed his fiddle case in the coffin and shot out the door past them. The piece of paper was still on the chair where he had been sitting.

'Strange lad,' said the man.

'Didn't even fill in his form,' said the woman.

'Funny black box,' said the man.

On the train Lenny relaxed. And as the wheels clattered out a rhythm, he perfected his wheeze for getting Scooby off his high horse and back into the team.

When Lenny walked into Sloggers' ground at 6.30 that evening the scoreboard told the sad, stark story. In the bottom frame it read 35, being what Lenny knew was the Sloggers' score. In the top frames it read 37 for 0. This meant Rycliffe had probably ended with a flourish in the form of a four. He braced himself for the darkness to come, but he bolstered himself to stand firm ... and then bring his rabbit out of the hat.

The whole team and Stan were hanging around near the pool table. Malcolm and Bal were having a half-hearted game. Lenny was glad to see that there was no sign of his parents.

Matey's was the first reaction. He pulled out the fines book and got as far as 'Leonard Henry Higgs, for dereliction of duty – ' before Roz stopped him.

'Sell many bats today?' she asked acidly. 'Your *mate*,' she spat the word out, 'wants the club to buy two.'

Lenny surprised them all by replacing his solemn look with a hefty grin. 'He's played right into my – I mean *our* hands – just give me five minutes of your time.'

They grumbled but, led by Donna and with Stan lending an ear from the edge, they listened, and, ten minutes later, from being cad of the week, Leonard Henry Higgs was flavour of the month.

By 7.15 Scooby Masters was standing by the pool table wearing a frown and listening to Stan's proposition.

'So having discussed all options with the team,' Stan sounded like the Mayor of Slogthwaite presiding over a big meeting, 'I, as manager, am making Norseman Products this proposal.' Lenny stood well out of Stan and Scooby's eye-line since he could scarcely stop laughing. Scooby looked like the boss of the Confederation of British Industry about to sell two nuclear power plants to Japan.

Stan spelt the plan out. 'Our two club bats are very tatty, so we would like to purchase from club funds,' the kids looked at each other in disbelief, what club funds? '... funds to be raised shortly – two Norseman bats.'

There was a solemn moment.

Scooby shut his eyes and steepled his fingers together. 'Wise, very wise.' He opened his eyes. 'As my partner, Lenny Higgs, and I can testify, these bats are the products of long, loving, expert endeavour. And their price is *usually* thirty-five pounds each. But since, judging by today's performance, you *need* my bats, I will sell them to Sloggers for sixty quid the pair.'

'Done,' said Stan. He shook Scooby's hand and there was a pathetic round of hand-clapping.

'One moment, partner.' Lenny's tone of half-sarcasm brought silence. 'Can we take it you will be showing us how to wield the Scooby Norseman in the six-a-side tournament on Saturday?'

'Certainly,' said Scooby. 'Now, I'm going to need this sixty pounds in full by next Saturday – or the deal's off.'

'You'll get it,' said Lenny with more confidence than anyone else felt.

On several fronts the next hour was one of the most

difficult that Lenny Higgs had ever negotiated. During it he had to take his mother from A to Z along the emotional spectrum: from black rage to happy, shining serenity. Lenny entered the house just after eight and got, as expected, a vintage mouthful.

Di ranted on about reliability, respectability, and self-respect. Barry sat throughout this with a mild, puzzled frown. When his mother had finished Lenny drew in his breath very calmly.

'All you say is right, Mum. But some people will say that my *end* justified my rather unorthodox means.'

Di's mouth began to flap but Barry held up a warning finger. 'You've had your say, Di, let Lenny have his.'

'I went off today to lull Scooby into a false sense of security,' said Lenny. 'I knew it was only a friendly game, so it didn't matter if we got pasted. Well, Scooby's only reaction was to say that if Sloggers bought two of his bats, for sixty quid, he would rejoin the team.' Lenny laughed. 'So with *your* help, Mum, we can get Sloggers back to winning ways.'

Di looked puzzled but Barry was all smiles. 'Well, I'll start the ball rolling, with twenty pounds I've raised on the teas.'

'And there's two pounds ten pence in the fines kitty,' said Lenny.

'So how do we raise the other thirty-seven pounds ninety pence?' asked Di.

Lenny looked archly at his father. 'Well, Mum, you've heard of sponsored swims, runs and walks. We just decided down at Sloggers to ask a very talkative member of the club to go on a week's sponsored *silence*.'

The word hung in the twilight air. Lenny kept his eyes on his dad. Lenny pulled a bag of coins out of his pocket. 'I've already got twelve pounds pledged if *you* can be silent from now until noon next Saturday, Mum.'

Di's expression defied description. Lenny put another two pound coins in the bag. Barry did the same. The Barnsley lip trembled and was about to flap.

'Sssh, Mum. The countdown started thirty seconds ago.'

Di's cheeks popped and her eyes rolled. Lenny and Barry, with great effort, kept their faces straight.

In the week that followed one or two folk took extreme advantage of Di's enforced silence.

Midweek found her outside a newsagent's in Crawford Street just as the afternoon edition of the *Dobcroft Gazette* was hitting the news-stands. Bal, Malcolm and Jason were reading the cricket as Di walked into the shop. They ran outside and began to laugh. Yorkshire had been beaten by Lancashire by nine wickets.

Bal's voice echoed into the shop. 'Ee by gum and hecky-peck, them Yorkies will be crying in their ale toneet. Thrashed . . .'

'Walloped,' said Malcolm.

'Humiliated, it says here,' yelled Jason.

Di ran out and waved her arms at them.

'Read all about it, Mrs Higgs,' said Bal thrusting the paper into her hands. She scrunched it up and stuffed it amongst the cans and chip-paper in a waste bin. The lads ran off laughing. Di choked down her rage.

The high point came at the supermarket on Friday night, only a matter of hours before the sponsored silence was due to end. Di was rooting around in some tins of beans and Geoffrey was sitting in the trolley covering his face with Twix. Pat Masters, wearing a pink cape and matching everything, tiptoed up and began wiping Geoffrey's face on a tissue.

'Mummy left you all mucky, has she?' Pat's voice could have been heard twenty metres away at the check-out. Di returned to the trolley, put some tins inside and began to wheel on. Pat restrained her. Her cheesy false grin widened. She took a fiver from her handbag. 'Do put this towards the cause.' For a tick Di seemed about to stick the money in Pat's ear. But she pocketed it and moved on.

A couple of hours later Lenny and Scooby were in the shed at Norseman Products. Lenny sat almost lovingly putting stickers on Norseman Two. Scooby swung Norseman One lustily, eager to get on the pitch in the six-a-side next day.

'So what's the line-up for the six-a-side, skip?' Scooby placed the bat carefully on the work bench.

Lenny did not look up. 'Roz, me, yourself, Bugle, Malcolm, Jason.'

'I expect you and me will open – with the new bats.' There was no way Scooby meant this as a question.

Lenny kept his eyes firmly fixed on the stickers on the bat. He did not want Scooby to twig that a plot was afoot to sabotage his dreams of fortune.

'Well, no,' said Lenny crisply. 'I thought you could stand by our stall, shout the odds, take orders, as me and Roz cream the ball to all parts of Sloggers' ground.' Out of the corner of his eye he could see that Scooby was buying this idea wholesale. 'Then you can come in, say number four, and crash it round.'

'Ace idea,' said Scooby. A slight edge of doubt filtered into the voice. 'The sixty quid is in the kitty, is it? No pay, no play, José.'

'I don't think my mum's efforts will have raised much less than that. You'd be amazed how many people like seeing other people get what they deserve.' Lenny stressed the last words.

Scooby reached for the switch on the Anglepoise lamp. 'We'll call it a draw now, partner.'

'No, you get off. I've got a few finishing touches to apply.'

Scooby left. With an evil grin Lenny reached for a small saw and began Operation Sink Scooby.

NINE

A small crowd had gathered inside the gate at Sloggers to see the end of Di's sponsored silence. Kids from the seven other cricket clubs involved in the six-a-side swelled the ranks of the locals. Stan had put his best suit on for the occasion, and Lenny and Scooby stood proudly in whites by the Norseman Products' stall. Lenny did not want Scooby to see the extra-large stickers he had plastered over the splice.

Stan coughed to get attention. 'Er – ladies and gentlemen, young cricketers, friends, before the first match in our tournament today we have a short ceremony.' Scooby looked like the cat that got the cream. He offered a high-five to Lenny; Lenny refused.

Stan continued. 'Sloggers decided recently to invest,' Stan nearly choked on the word, 'in two Norseman bats from Timothy Masters...'

Scooby leaned over and whispered something in Stan's ear. Stan bridled then spat out, 'Managing Director of Norseman Products.'

Matey pushed his way to the front with a shoebox full of notes and coins. He was not looking happy.

'We have raised sixty pounds, mainly by a sponsored silence kindly achieved by Mrs Di Higgs. So give her a big hand, she's not said a peep for a week.' Stan led the strong applause.

Barry kissed Di. Matey dived into urgent discussion with Stan. Stan's face darkened.

'Er, ladies and gents,' said Stan meekly. 'I'm afraid there's a rabbit off here.' He looked sadly at Di. 'You've done your best, Mrs H, but we're five quid short of the sixty notes.'

Scooby blenched. He tried to take the bats from Lenny but could not. 'Full cash or no bash,' shouted Scooby.

There was a movement in the crowd. It parted to let through Mr Ackroyd. He pointed his walking-stick at Di. 'Is it right that yon woman has not opened her gob for a whole week?'

'Correct,' said Stan.

Mr Ackroyd pulled a crumpled fiver from his overcoat pocket. 'Well, put this in the kitty. Are you sure you don't want a tenner?'

Applause swelled. Scooby took the money and went behind the stall to count it.

Stan turned to Di. 'You're the heroine of the week, Di. Speech?'

Di shook her head. The kids applauded like mad.

Lenny walked off, carrying the two bats as if they were the crown jewels.

'Play all your shots, partner,' Scooby shouted.

'Oh, I will, I surely will,' Lenny called back to him.

The first match in the tournament was Sloggers against Daisy Bank. Lenny won the toss and decided to bat. As the Daisy Bank fielders positioned themselves, Lenny seemed almost reluctant to hand over the Norseman bat to Roz.

'I know these matches are slogging jobs, Lenny,' whined Roz. 'But at least let me get a feel of the bat.'

Lenny held one bat by the bottom of the blade. He gently passed the other to Roz. He whispered in her ear and she burst into hysterical laughter. With all eyes on them – Scooby, Stan, the Higgs family, and the rest of the team – they carried the bats like two arms-bearers approaching knights ready to joust.

Scooby laid on the sales patter. 'First-ever live demo of the bats they're all talking about from the Oval to Orinoco...'

Zoë, Bal, Matey and Bugle stood by Scooby's stall as the Daisy Bank bowler ran in. Roz at the non-striker's end suddenly played a practice hook – and the blade flew off the handle of the bat. Lenny smacked the ball to the boundary – and the bat's blade followed. Lenny and

Roz waved the handles at each other like apprentice fencers.

Sporadic laughter broke out. All the adults except Stan and Barry were struck dumb. Scooby looked like Sylvester after taking a cannonball in the face from Tweety Pie.

'Con artist!' Matey screeched as he reclaimed the box of cash.

'Shoddy goods and no mistake', said Bal.

Zoë's face had turned pink. 'I say, teach this fraud a lesson.' She began to push at Norseman Products' stall. Bugle and a gang of others helped. Scooby stood aghast. He did not lift so much as a finger to try to stop them.

Suddenly Bugle bent into the wreckage of the stall. He picked up a brown cardboard box. He dipped inside and pulled out a large stand pie.

'The Pie Piper,' said Bugle in awe. 'At least *his* products are the business.'

The next few days should have been happy ones for Lenny. Everyone thought his way of teaching Scooby a lesson had been brill. And Scooby himself, with his hide like a rhino, bounced back. He announced the end of his business career and began batting really well in the mid-week nets. Lenny's form had gone completely. But what was really on his mind was the orchestra. Nearly two weeks had passed since the audition and he had heard nothing. Nor could he chat things over with Dot Ball or Donna. Dot was in the south on holiday for a fortnight and Donna seemed preoccupied by something or other. Roz kept giving him google-eyes, but his mood was anything but romantic.

Now it was tea-time on Friday and Lenny was preparing his kit for a key match the next day against Dobcroft. He sat in the kitchen putting oil on his best bat. The phone extension in the hall rang.

Lenny was there like a flash. If it's the orchestra lot I'll play it dead cool, he determined. 'Hello, hello, Leonard

Higgs.' It was not about music. It was Mrs Sykes, a friend of Di's who had just been on a visit to Barnsley.

Glumly Lenny called for his mother and handed over the phone. Lenny got back to his oiling as his mum twittered, but then he noticed an urgency and excitement come into her voice.

'A scout. A Yorkshire cricket scout. Coming over here ... tomorrow!' Di was now boogying round the hall. Lenny felt no buzz at all. He was batting like a drain so it was no time to be put under the microscope. His mother put the phone down with a clatter.

'That was Leanne Sykes. The word from Barnsley is that Yorkshire scouts are scouring the north looking for lads.' Di was bouncing up and down. 'Somebody has mentioned your name. And a scout could be at Sloggers tomorrow.'

Lenny managed a weak smile. 'Great, Mum. Fill him up with some of Dad's tea delicacies and I'll be reporting to Headingley on Monday.'

Di frowned, realising that the news had not exactly sent Lenny over the moon. She opened her mouth as Barry walked in.

'I'd have thought such news would have made your day, L. H. Higgs,' she said sharply. 'Oh, Barry love, wait till you hear the news...'

'No need, darling,' Barry laughed. 'I've been ear-wigging the phone call. And it's great.'

Di glared at Lenny. 'So why does our son look so mealy-mouthed?'

Barry looked at his watch. 'Weren't you due at the hairdresser's five minutes ago, dear?'

Di gasped. 'You're right.'

'I suggest you shoot off then. We can't have the Yorkshire scout reporting that the batting star's mum has rat's tails.'

Di bolted.

Geoffrey came into the kitchen with his plastic bat and Barry began bowling at him.

'Want to tell your dad what's on your mind?' asked Barry quietly.

Lenny composed his thoughts for a minute. 'It's not that I'm not keen to go as far as I can with cricket, Dad. But it's been nearly two weeks since I auditioned for the youth orchestra and I've not heard a dicky-bird.'

Barry patted him playfully on the head. 'So that's the weight you've been carrying. Look, I've got some pals at the poly with music contacts. I'll get them to make a few calls on Monday.'

'Great if you would, Dad.'

Barry bowled a dolly at Geoffrey. He whacked it into the hall. 'So why don't you concentrate on tomorrow's game? Get yer 'ead down, our Leonard.'

I will, but the strokes might not come, thought Lenny.

Before the Higgs family left the house just after 1 p.m. the next day there was the usual mad panic. Di normally made efforts to dress up after a new hair-do, but today she was in a Yorkshire County Cricket Club track suit and wearing a bobble hat to match.

'Don't you think that's OTT, Mum?' pleaded Lenny.

'I'm proud to be a Yorkie,' roared Di as she helped Barry pack the tea stuff. 'You go and make sure your kit is in A1 order.'

Lenny looked out the kitchen window at the back garden. The bright sun gleamed off the mini-sightscreen at the canal end; the grass of the 'wicket' was a worn faded yellow. Oh, to be out there playing cricket for fun instead of in the glare of public and professional scrutiny . . .

'Frame yourself, our Leonard,' came his mother's voice.

Lenny grabbed viciously at the handle of his coffin and reeled backwards as the handle lost contact with the box. It took another five minutes of scrabbling while his mother rattled on at him before his gear was repacked in an old canvas holdall.

It was 1.15 before the Higgses were in the car and hurtling to the ground. No phone call; no confidence; no Donna to talk to and now I'll be fined for being late. I think I'll take up sommat peaceful and non-traumatic like bullfighting, thought Lenny.

In fact several others of the Sloggers' team were also late.

Matey and Bal rushed through the gate and almost knocked over a grey-haired man in his early sixties, very smartly dressed in a suit and tie.

'Sorry, pal,' said Bal.

The stranger peered at them with a polite smile. He seemed very interested in Matey's canvas cricket bag. On the side in white was lettered 'Adam Tait. Slogthwaite CC'.

'Nay, lads, don't apologise, get on with thee laiking.'

'German, I'd say,' said Matey.

'Funny fella,' said Bal.

The two lads rushed towards the changing rooms.

The stranger almost had a wobbler when he spied Scooby coming through the gate with his state-of-the-art coffin. Scooby's had his name and club in gold Gothic script: 'Timothy Vernon Masters. Slogthwaite CC. Founded 1837'.

'Hey up, young man, 'appen you've a 'alf mo for a bit of a chat?' The man was half-bent in supplication.

'If you're an investment broker or owt like that you can forget it, pal. My business career is on hold. Ta-ra.' Scooby hurried off across the grass.

Lenny breezed in through the gates. As usual the physical impact of walking into the historic ground and sensing the great feats performed there stimulated him. Today, I'm going to get runs...

A man a bit over-dressed for cricket-watching nodded to him.

'Hey up,' said the stranger.

'Hey up,' replied Lenny cheerfully.

Di came in next, she and Geoffrey loaded with bags and tins.

'Hey up, missus, tha's looking full o' busy.' The stranger smiled at Di.

She jerked bolt upright. Barry came in behind her and Di off-loaded most of her stuff. 'Tek this lot, Barry. I think *this* is our man.'

Barry rolled his eyes. Goodness knows what Di can burble into the scout's ear in the forty minutes before the game started, he thought. She can probably wreck Lenny's chances with Yorkshire before they can get started.

'Hello there,' said Barry politely to the stranger.

'Hey up,' said the stranger.

'I'm sure our Yorkshire friend here is gaspin' for a brew. Get t'kettle on, our Baz.' Di was in full song.

Cringing at the prospect of Di talking the man to death, Barry led Geoffrey off to the tea-room.

'My name's Higgs. Originally from Barnsley. You can call me Di.' Di held out her right hand.

The stranger took it timidly. 'Hargreaves. Gordon Hargreaves. I'm from Scarborough. Look – er, Di – I'm looking for a special case . . .'

'Case, special case,' Di laughed. 'We've got all sorts here. Nut cases. Hard cases. But *show* cases are our speciality. My son Lenny is a brilliant batter. Come and have a cup of tea and I'll tell you all about him.'

'If you don't mind I'll take up that offer later,' came the reply.

Hargreaves moved off towards the old seat. Steady as she goes, said Di to herself. I'll play my cards clever and catch Mr Hargreaves when Lenny is on full song. She headed for the tea-room.

After a short team talk on the importance of winning and going to the top of the league, Stan followed Lenny into the middle for the toss.

'It's up to you, Len, but if I won the toss I'd bat,' murmured Stan.

Lenny nodded his agreement.

A group of people were on the square apparently sussing out the state of the surface. Di was on her hands and knees. Roz was at the other end peering at the grass. Dobcroft's big-headed skipper, Ian Battersby, stood waiting for Lenny with a smug look. Donna stood about a metre away from Ian with a funny look in her eyes.

Di, as usual, was anything but subtle as Lenny brought out a coin and prepared to toss. 'You should field first if you get the chance, Leonard.' Roz, Donna and Ian looked askance. Stan snorted. Di continued, 'Let Dobby get a ton or so, then show us some strokes.' She nodded and winked at Lenny like an idiot. She pointed to Hargreaves who was now standing by the old seat. 'Yorkshire scout,' she mouthed.

Lenny looked Battersby firmly in the face. 'Call,' he said and flipped the coin.

'If it's OK with your advisers,' said Ian sarcastically, 'I'll have tails.'

The coin came down tails.

'We'll *bat*,' said Ian. He gave an exaggerated wink to Donna then ran off. Lenny wasn't sure but he thought Donna blushed a little.

'Don't tire yourself in the field, our Leonard,' shouted Di as she made off towards the old seat.

'Mum,' yelled Lenny, 'there's more than me playing this game.'

'Steady on,' said Roz as she followed him off. 'Is that man really a Yorkshire scout?'

'I don't care if he's an alien from Planet Zog, can we just get on and play cricket,' screamed Lenny.

TEN

The Dobcroft openers, Ian Battersby and Ronnie Moss, started off ultra-cautiously. They were very respectful of both Malcolm's and Slasher's first two overs. With the score standing at 10 for 0, the batters had a mid-square conference and Lenny urged on his troops.

'On yer toes, Sloggers. Fire it in, Malc,' shouted Lenny.

Donna was standing next to Lenny in the slips. 'Knock this fella's poles over, Malc.' Ian Battersby, preparing to take strike, turned, winked and blew her a kiss.

'Take no notice of this poser,' yelled Lenny. But what's that funny look in Donna's eyes all about? he wondered.

The ball from Malcolm was a wicked bouncer. Ian skilfully angled it down to Donna's left. She dived and stopped a certain four. All the Sloggers' lot applauded. Ian pounded his bat on his glove.

'Great stop, darlin',' he shouted.

'Less of the good sport nonsense, Batters, get your mind on the game,' roared Ronnie from the other end.

Ian played the next few balls sensibly.

On the boundary near the old seat Scooby was looking forward to batting. At this rate Dobby will only get around a hundred and ten, and the wicket's perfect, he mused. Me and Len will cruise it.

'Er, young man, er, I wonder if you mind me asking you something?' It was the stranger with the Yorkshire accent.

In the middle Slasher was having trouble with his run-up, and in the lull Scooby turned round.

The man fiddled with his specs. 'That black box of yours. I suppose you keep a lot of different things in it?'

'Yeah,' said Scooby derisively. 'There's me sandwiches. The Good Food Guide. And sometimes our budgie, when I take him for a walk and he gets tired.'

The ball flew from Ronnie's bat along the ground to Scooby's left. He raced to it, dipped, scooped it up and hurled it in to Bugle. The batters forgot about a second run. Sloggers applauded the throw.

Di sidled up to Hargreaves. She pointed to Scooby.

'Great arm, that lad,' said Di.

'Arm?' asked Hargreaves.

'Ball straight to the stumper.' Di this time with a note of impatience.

'Stumper?' asked Hargreaves.

'Oh I see, playing the innocent.' Di began to walk away. 'Oh, watch the Sloggers' captain, Leonard Higgs. Great bat, great fielder.'

In the middle Ronnie lunged forward. The ball got an edge and flew low to Lenny.

He got a hand to it, but the ball bobbled on to the grass.

'Rubbish, our Lenny, that was a dolly,' screamed Di.

'Dolly?' asked Hargreaves.

'Very difficult to catch,' rapped Di. She moved on round the boundary. I might have to leave impressing Mr Hargreaves to our Leonard, she thought.

Half an hour later Dobcroft were looking increasingly more dangerous. They had progressed to 53 for 1. Ronnie Moss was out, but Ian Battersby was starting to play his shots. Lenny had the bulk of his fielders out on the boundary.

Inside the tea-room Pat Masters was watching the game through the window, as Barry finished setting out the tea stuff.

'Another four,' sighed Pat. 'I hope our batters are in good nick.'

Barry joined her at the window. Geoffrey played happily, practising bowling at the tea-counter. 'I hope Dobby don't get much more than a hundred. Scooby's in good form but our Lenny's completely lost confidence. He'll have to work for every run today.'

A rather untidy man walked into the tea-room. He looked older than he probably was. He wore a flat hat, a raincoat and was carrying a shopping bag. Pat curled up her nose. But Barry, never one to pre-judge people, gave the stranger a friendly nod.

'Any chance of a drop of tea?' asked the newcomer.

Pat frowned. No tea was usually sold until the end of the innings. Barry was all smiles. He made for the boiler behind the counter. The man took a battered old Thermos flask from his bag.

'I like supping tea while I watch cricket. Can you fill this up? No sugar. Only a drop o' milk.' The voice was Northern, quiet and polite.

Barry filled the flask and took fifty pence from the man. 'Are you a Dobby supporter?'

The man grinned. 'No. I'm just a cricket bloke. Can I get a pie at half-time?'

'No. We're taking tea at the end today. Both teams agree,' said Barry. 'But I'll keep you a growler.'

'Fine,' said the man. 'Oh, who's batting?'

'Dobcroft,' said Pat. 'Going well, but we'll beat them.'

'Funny game, cricket,' said the man. 'You never know what's going to happen.'

The stranger left the tea-room and walked slowly towards the old seat.

Mr Ackroyd was sitting peacefully and there was no sign of Mr Hargreaves. The stranger poured himself a cup of tea from the flask and began sipping as Zoë lobbed a sitter up to Ian. The ball was crisply dispatched to the boundary. Di stopped less than a metre away from the stranger.

'Good shot, lad,' said the stranger. 'Right off the meat of the bat.'

Di drew herself to her full height. She sneered at the stranger. 'Meat! Meat! That was more off the scrag-end if you ask me. Spawniest shot I've seen in a while that!'

'Rubbish,' said the man.

'You Dobby supporters are all the same. Biased, big-mouthed and *blind*.' She pointed at the shopping bag. 'Got your white stick hidden in there, have you?'

With that Di stormed off. The stranger smiled and continued supping tea.

It was time for the last over of the Dobcroft innings, and Sloggers were in trouble. The score was 130 for 5 and Ian was still in. He had anchored the innings and got forty-six runs but was now set to slog.

Lenny had the ball and was having a quiet conference with Roz.

'We don't want Batters cracking a dozen off this over,' said Roz.

'But who can I put on to bowl?' Lenny scanned the troops. Nobody was going through the motions of turning their arm over. 'Malcolm's tired. Slasher's bottled out. Zoë's too hittable.'

Lenny's eye fell on Donna. She would not meet it. 'Ian's been teasing Donna all game. He's trying to put her off...'

'Or he fancies her,' said Roz.

'Don't be daft. He's from Dobby,' rasped Lenny. 'I'll put her on. It might just faze him.'

He beckoned Donna over and a buzz went round the ground.

''Ere, girl, line and length.' Lenny lobbed the ball gently to Donna. She was so surprised she missed it.

Giggles went up from the Dobcroft kids. 'Whack it, Batters. It's yer birthday, fella.'

Ian settled at the crease, but did not look happy. Suddenly Ronnie Moss's voice echoed out. 'Head not heart, Ian. Give her the treatment.'

Roz turned to Lenny in the strips. 'It's just like I thought. Donna and Ian have got a thing going.'

'Stop being Marjorie Proops, and concentrate,' hissed Lenny.

Donna's first two balls were on a good length. Ian tried to straight-drive but each hit was firmly collected by Donna. The Dobcroft lot seethed. 'Come on, Ian, give it some clog!'

Donna pitched the next ball up a bit. Ian did well to block it.

'Rubbish, Batters,' yelled Ronnie. 'Hit out or get out.'

Ian was now seething. He did not bother with a guard. He stood like a baseball batter. He took two wild swipes at Donna's next two balls – and missed.

'Keep it there,' yelled Lenny jubilantly.

Donna tried to fool Ian with the last ball of the innings. She bowled it slower. He whacked it back at her at nose height. She raised her hands, missed and the ball hurtled to the boundary.

Dobcroft went wild. Sloggers applauded Ian's fifty. He raised his bat, and gave a silly mock bow to Donna. She went beetroot.

One hundred and thirty-four went up in the frame for Dobcroft.

'Well bowled,' said Lenny. 'You did try to catch that last one, didn't you?'

Donna paused. 'Course I did. Why on earth would I let it go? Think I'm stupid?'

She ran off towards the tea-room.

After drinks and a short team talk Lenny and Scooby went out to bat. Stan had said the way to get 135 was for Lenny to hold one end and Scooby to go for the runs. So tough luck on the Yorkshire scout, thought Lenny, he'll see no shots from me. I'm playing for the team today.

As he walked out to open the innings with Scooby, Lenny noticed the scout standing by the old seat talking to Bugle. A couple of metres along the boundary was another stranger in a flat hat. In between them stood Di. Oh, please keep it buttoned, Mum, thought Lenny.

'Give it some pasty, Scooby,' yelled Bugle.

'Pasty?' asked Hargreaves.

'Welly. Tap. Big licks,' Bugle explained as if the man was daft.

The first twenty minutes of the innings went well for Sloggers. Scooby played in cavalier fashion and cruised to twenty-five. Lenny prodded and plodded. He was happy to nudge the odd single. Even Di saw the sense of this so, for the moment, kept mum. Sloggers needed ninety runs off twenty overs.

Dobcroft were trying all the tricks. Ian and Ronnie kept up a constant stream of chat to Lenny. 'Hit it, Higgsy, it won't hurt you,' and the like. Lenny took no notice. He kept his head down and grafted. Then a ball from Ronnie sat and begged to be hit. Lenny creamed it for four to the old seat.

Di broke into rapturous applause.

To her left the stranger with the shopping bag applauded. 'Now that was a good shot, missus. And that lad is playing right in his head. Truly an innings the team need.'

Di was amazed. Sense. Good sound sense. 'Thanks, that lad's my son. Nice to have appreciation from a Dobby supporter.'

The stranger appeared to be about to reply, but instead took out his flask of tea. In the middle Scooby swept to forty-four.

It was all going beautifully, with Lenny trying a few shots, and the team were on 74 for 0, when Scooby went for a six. He was brilliantly caught on the boundary. He shrugged to Lenny and walked off to cheers. Scooby had scored fifty-five, Lenny fifteen, and there were four extras.

There were twelve overs to go and off them Sloggers needed sixty-one runs. It should be on, thought Lenny, but if Roz gets out we're in trouble.

He called a mid-pitch conflab when Roz arrived on the square.

'Should I have a go or will you?' asked Lenny.

Roz tossed her head. 'I'll go after them, you're doing a

great job as the anchor.' She paused. 'If I get fifty will you take me out for a burger tonight?'

Lenny laughed. 'If you get fifty, girl, I'll buy you burgers for life!'

'Get on with it,' yelled Ian.

Roz gave him a look of pure venom. She took guard.

In the next half-hour Roz Crabtree batted brilliantly. She cut, hooked and drove all that Dobcroft could offer. Lenny loosened up at the other end and tickled a couple of twos down to fine leg. A four off a tired Ronnie Moss took Roz to fifty. Lenny was on twenty-two. Sloggers were on 131 and needed only four runs to win.

Roz faced the last ball of Ronnie's over. Eager to win the match with a four she lofted her drive and was caught. She was given a great ovation.

There were three overs left and Sloggers had a tent full of batters. Donna walked slowly to the crease, eyes down.

'Donna,' hissed Lenny. 'Let's do it in singles.'

She bit her lip and nodded.

Ian Battersby stood with the ball. He knew his team had no hope.

'I'll bowl,' he announced loudly.

'Might have known,' yelled Ronnie. 'He'll bowl a sweetheart ball to his rotten sweetheart.'

Donna turned crimson. Lenny scratched his head. So Roz's instinct had been spot on.

'Don't try nowt silly,' shouted Lenny.

Aware that his relationship with Donna was now being blamed for the game going against his team, Ian tried to bowl a yorker. The ball, instead, became a full toss. Donna walloped it over Ian's head for four. There was no need to run.

The Dobcroft team left the field in silence – except for Ian. He shook Lenny's hand. 'Good game. Well batted, Higgsy.'

Ian turned to Donna. He shook her hand.

'Why not give her a kiss and be done with it,' asked Lenny with a twinkle.

Lenny walked off the pitch feeling good. So what if his mum *did* say you should have done this for the scout or that for the scout . . . Sloggers had won. He also had twenty-two not out in the book, and a date for the night.

Lenny fought his way through the throng in the tearoom. He could see Dot Ball near the door. He held high his plate of food and cup of tea. Dot was looking very tanned from her holiday. She was talking to Donna, with Ian in smiling attendance.

'Hello, Lenny,' said Dot. 'Well batted. That puts us top of the league, doesn't it?'

'Certainly does,' said Lenny with a friendly sneer to Ian.

Mr Hargreaves came bustling in the door. He saw Di making for him and froze. Dot Ball tapped his shoulder. 'Gordon Hargreaves, what are you doing at a cricket match?'

The words stopped all conversation near the door.

Hargreaves took off his glasses and wiped them on his hanky. 'Dot, thank heavens and what a relief. Somebody who will not rail on at me about pasties, taps, dollies and so on. It's been like visiting a foreign land.'

This did not seem like talk appropriate to a Yorkshire cricket scout. Other folk crowded round.

'So why are you here, Gordon?' asked Dot.

'Well, as you know, Dot, I am well thought of in certain music circles.' A buzz went round the room. Di's face began to colour. Lenny felt a small steel spring begin to coil in his stomach. 'And recently I was asked to help in the formation of a Lancashire Youth Orchestra.' Dot looked warmly at Lenny. Donna dug him in the back. Lenny could not take his eyes off Mr Hargreaves. 'Two weeks ago we held auditions and my colleagues heard a very good boy violinist . . .' The next words were

119

drowned in hubbub. All of Sloggers knew who the phantom fiddler would be.

Hargreaves realised he had an audience. 'Well, the boy was so nervous, and in such a hurry, that he did not fill in the forms. All we knew was he brought his violin in a curious black box that mentioned Slogthwaite Cricket Club...'

Dot stopped him. 'Allow me to introduce your phantom fiddler – this is Leonard Higgs.'

Everybody broke into spontaneous applause – apart from Di. She looked about to burst into tears when the stranger in the flat cap with the shopping bag walked in and joined Scooby and Pat Masters.

Di's voice shook the plate-glass windows. 'Well, if this fellow is a fiddle scout, who is he?' She pointed to the stranger.

The stranger doffed his cap. 'My name is George Rimmer, love. And I do a bit of scouting for Yorkshire cricket.'

The whole room was stunned. Only Donna and Lenny found the situation funny. Di marched over to Rimmer.

'Why didn't you tell us who you were?' she demanded.

'Because nobody asked, and I'm not sure I'd have let on anyroad.' He turned to Scooby. 'I came specifically to watch Leonard Higgs, but you took the honours today, young man. Would you come to nets in Yorkshire if asked?'

It was too much for Di. 'Hang on. My lad didn't do all that bad today – and he was *born* in Yorkshire.'

Pat Masters was in like a shot. 'Oh, but hang on yourself, Di Higgs. I'll have you know that Scooby was born in Saddlewarth when it was part of Yorkshire. So...'

'So, calm down, ladies,' said Rimmer. 'Are you interested in this year, Scooby? And are you interested for next year, Lenny?'

Scooby pondered for a second or two. 'I'm not sure I want to play for the Yorkies. Can you wait till I have words with Old Trafford?'

'I'll come to nets next year, if asked,' said Lenny.

Di was about to have her twopennyworth but Barry led her and Lenny into a corner.

'So, what say fiddle for Lancashire this year, cricket for Yorkshire next year, when our kid's an old man of fifteen?' Barry stared Di down.

'OK,' she said. 'It's a deal.'

'Barry,' came a mournful cry from the food-counter. 'Any more nosh?' Bugle, Jason and Slasher were standing like Oliver Twist and his buddies.

Barry looked downcast. He walked to the counter. 'Nowt left. Sorry, kids.'

Balwinder slipped behind a pile of chairs. He came out with a giant cardboard box. 'I wonder what's in here?' he asked.

He opened the lid and took out a slice of pork pie. Bugle tasted it. 'Delicious.'

Bal slid out a massive stand pie, half a metre in diameter.

'The Pie Piper has done it again,' said Jason in awe.

Hargreaves had come up on them quietly. 'May I try a piece of that pie?'

Jason offered him a slice. Hargreaves bit off a corner and chewed. 'Perfect,' he said. 'Crust not soggy. Meat to jelly ratio spot on. Very unusual herbs...'

'That's the secret,' yelled Bal. 'Put in a touch of marjoram, bit of basil, and just a pinch of pepper. Don't overcook the meat and always grease the tin properly so the crust doesn't stick.'

The silence lasted ten seconds. 'So you, Balwinder Singh, are the Pie Piper,' said Zoë.

Bal looked sheepish. 'Well, not exactly, I'm like his apprentice. The real boss man is...'

'Thomas Ackroyd, master butcher.' Mr Ackroyd elbowed his way to the front. 'I won every pie fair from

Ramsbottom to the Rhineland in my time. And young Bal here has helped me keep my hand in. We thought we'd thank you – me for the cricket, him for the special teas – and we thought we'd kid you on a bit. It were nowt but 'armless fun.'

Lenny called for three cheers for the Pie Piper and his apprentice.

It had been a rare day for surprises at Sloggers, and they were not over. People were starting to drift away from the tea-counter when Stan clapped his hands for order.

'I have a special announcement to make,' said Stan sheepishly.

Len turned to Roz with a puzzled frown. 'You don't think he's going to make Scooby captain?'

Roz squeezed his hand reassuringly. 'No chance. Scoob's too full of himself. You'll be skipper next year.'

Stan spoke louder. 'Next year there will be challenges anew to face. We've got to keep Jason's head out of the horoscope pages and Lenny off the fiddle long enough to anchor our batting...' There was a bit of joky jeering.

'But there will be one important change in our setup.' Stan looked serious. The mood of the company changed. The kids looked worried. Stan moved from the counter and stood beside Di. She must have sensed something fateful was about to happen because she tugged off her bobble hat and frizzed up her hair.

Stan placed his hand gently on Di's shoulder. 'I have been junior manager for donkey's years now. So I am stepping down next season. And I am proposing that Mrs Di Higgs takes my place.'

The audience could not have been more astonished if Michael Jackson had walked in and asked for a pork pie.

'Mega-revolutionary,' said Jason.

'Dictatorship,' hissed Malcolm.

'Ecky thump,' gasped Bal.

Di flushed, gasped and wiped away a genuine tear. 'I –

I – I – don't know what to say, Stan. But I accept.' She kissed Stan on the forehead. 'I promise I will maintain your modest, firm attitude. I won't change a thing.'

'I'll bet,' said Lenny.

By eight o'clock Lenny and Roz had finished their burgers and were walking along Green Lane. Roz was on cloud nine and Lenny was rapturous to have all his worries about cricket and music removed from his life.

They were level with the score-box at Sloggers' ground. Lenny put his arm round Roz's shoulders and was trying to think up something romantic to say. Then a too-well-known voice echoed from over the wall.

'Mine! All mine!'

The two kids froze. Then they began to giggle softly. They peeked over the wall.

Di was striding along the boundary waving her arms. 'I have a dream,' she echoed. 'Hospitality suites. Facilities for parascending, electronic scoreboard – we'll burn that old heap of rubbish. Now where will we put the press...'

Lenny and Roz bobbed down.

'Here we go again,' said Lenny.

'As the old saying goes,' said Roz sagely. 'There's many a slip 'twixt cup and lip.'

''Appen,' said Lenny.

Beginner's Guide to Sloggers' Jargon

beck – stream
chelp – nag
cow-shot – wild swipe
dolly – easy
frame yourself – get your act together
full monty – dressed to kill
full toss – ball that does not bounce
gobslotches – fools
growler – pork pie
keep a monk on – sulk
knock – absent
jocks – runs
laik – play
Lankie – person from Lancashire
noddles – heads
pasty – power
slog – wild swipe
sloughened off – cheesed off
spawny – lucky
tap – hard hit
thrape – swipe
tin-lad – scorer's apprentice
waft – loose shot
wassock – fool
yahoo – wild swipe

Main Fielding Positions

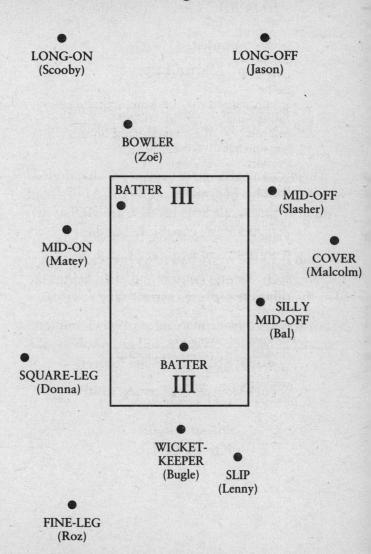

The Boot Street Band
Steve Attridge
Based on the BBC TV series by
Andrew Davies & Steve Attridge

The members of Class 4D at Boot Street School
are definitely different from other school-
children. Since their teacher (now believed to be
somewhere in Fiji) walked out to fetch a rubber
last November, they have managed very nicely
on their own. In fact, they now manage the
entire school with a little help from Mr Prince,
whose bark is worse than his bite, and no help
at all from Mr Lear, the headmaster, who is
quite obviously barmy. But Boot Street School,
the centre of 4D's profit-making recycling
empire and the sole producer of National
Curriculum toilet rolls, is threatened with
closure and it is up to 'The Management'
of 4D to save it or lose everything . . .

The Byker Grove series

Byker Grove
Adele Rose

Heartbreak for Donna
Carrie Rose

Odd Ones Out
James Weir

Turning On, Tuning In
Don Webb

Green for Danger
Don Webb

Love Without Hope
Wally K Daly

Fighting Back
Wally K Daly

Temptation
Wally K Daly

The Dark House
Don Webb